"I want to
Benedict

He stood in the ... ...ng room, dark and brooding and thoroughly dominating.

"Where is she?" he demanded, looking around the room as if expecting to find Sammi tucked up on the sofa.

"Benedict," Verity said in a soft, protective voice. "Sammi is sound asleep and she has school in the morning. If she is woken up in the middle of the night by a total..." She bit her lip and her words tailed off as she realized just what she had been about to say so tactlessly. And truthfully.

"Stranger?" he replied acidly.

Sharon Kendrick was born in West London and has had *heaps* of jobs, including photography, nursing, driving an ambulance across the Australian desert and cooking her way around Europe in a converted double-decker bus! Without a doubt, writing is the best job she has ever had, and when she's not dreaming up new heroes (some of which are based on her doctor husband!) she likes cooking, reading, theater, drinking wine, listening to American West Coast music and talking to her two children, Celia and Patrick.

Books by Sharon Kendrick

HARLEQUIN PRESENTS
1820—PART-TIME FATHER

Look out in March for *Taking It All* by Sharon Kendrick, the sequel to *Taking Risks*.

Taking Risks
Sharon Kendrick

Harlequin Books

TORONTO • NEW YORK • LONDON
AMSTERDAM • PARIS • SYDNEY • HAMBURG
STOCKHOLM • ATHENS • TOKYO • MILAN
MADRID • WARSAW • BUDAPEST • AUCKLAND

ISBN 0-373-17313-X

TAKING RISKS

First North American Publication 1997.

CHAPTER ONE

'I SUPPOSE it was inevitable, really.' Verity gave a heavy sigh as she stared into the full-length mirror which was *supposed* to add light and depth to a tiny sitting room which desperately needed both. But somehow the mirror had never quite achieved its purpose!

Butter-coloured curls were tossed as a small head was turned upwards and a pair of very big, very blue eyes widened into cornflower saucers. 'What's 'nevitable, Mummy?' The child concentrated fiercely on the new word and a pudgy little hand tugged at the hem of Verity's tartan miniskirt.

Verity turned away from the mirror and smiled with automatic pleasure as her eyes met those of her interested little daughter, her troubles momentarily forgotten as she thought for the hundredth time how adorable Sammi looked in her new school uniform. 'Nothing, darling,' she hedged. Why subject Sammi to fears which might not, after all, come to anything at all? 'Sammi mustn't worry.'

But Sammi was not to be deterred. She may not have anything of her father's looks about her, thought Verity with a grim kind of humour, but she had certainly inherited his determination!

The cornflower saucers were screwed up into

petal shapes as Sammi again tried to remember the word her mother had used. ''Nevitable!' she recalled, triumph curving her rosebud mouth. 'What's 'nevitable, Mummy?'

Verity was torn between fierce maternal pride at her five-year-old's vocabulary and the worry of how she was going to keep the momentous news from her.

That Benedict was about to re-enter her life.

Benedict Jackson—the hunky obstetrician and gynaecologist who could charm just about any woman he wanted with an irresistible combination of arrogance, wit and good old-fashioned sex appeal!

But how could you turn round to a five-year-old who, to all intents and purposes, believed that she *had* no father—and tell her that she had? And not only that. That the man in question was one of the finest surgeons in his field. The rising star of obstetrics and gynaecology, with more original research papers to his name than Verity had had hot dinners.

And that later on that morning she would be standing opposite him in the operating theatre, assisting the great man as his scrub nurse.

She had spent the last week wondering how on earth she was going to cope with working side by side with the father of her child. Especially when that man remained ignorant of his paternity.

Verity had also given considerable thought as to *why* Benedict was taking up the post of senior registrar at St Jude's. Oh, it was true that St Jude's, set in one of the prettiest parts of North London, was an internationally renowned hospital. But so, too, was the hospital in which the two of them had trained—Benedict as a doctor and Verity as a nurse. The prestigious St Thomas's on the other side of London—where generations of Jacksons had dominated the surgical wards. Benedict had fitted in well there, with most of the nurses madly in love with him and nearly all the doctors in awe of his father's reputation as dean of the medical school.

So why come here, of all places?

Oh, sweet mercy! Verity thought despairingly. The whole situation was like something out of her very worst nightmare, which had begun when she had picked up the off-duty last week and seen the new senior registrar's name.

Benedict Jackson.

It might as well have been written in letters of fire because she had dropped the off-duty on Sister's floor as though she had been burnt and Sister Saunders had given her a most peculiar look.

If only Jamie Brennan hadn't gone away on holiday, Verity sighed inwardly as she slicked some peach-coloured gloss over her full mouth. She always scrubbed for the popular young consultant herself, which meant that at least one of the junior staff nurses would have had the dubious pleasure of dealing with the new surgeon. And not her.

Or if only Jamie had mentioned the name of his new senior registrar to her before he had gone off to Florida then it might not have come as such a shock. But why would he do that? she reasoned. He certainly didn't name *all* the new members of medical staff who passed through the hospital under his superb tutelage. And it would not occur to him to mention Benedict in particular, despite his close relationship with Verity, since he had no idea that his new senior registrar was the father of her child.

No one did. Though many wondered. Just as they wondered about the true extent of the slim, blonde staff nurse's involvement with her consultant.

For Verity and Jamie were friends outside as well as inside work and that was official.

The two of them had worked side by side in Theatres for the four years that Verity had been at St Jude's. Jamie always said that she was the best scrub nurse he had ever had—apart from Kathy, of course—and he had married Kathy and forbidden her to ever work again!

He and Kathy had had a daughter, Harriet, who was just a year older than Sammi, and Verity and Jamie used to spend hours comparing notes over the operating table as they had each passed through the various stages of child-rearing. And although Jamie was a fairly conventional man, despite his relatively tender years, he had never once commented or judged Verity on her single-mother status and for that she had been eternally grateful.

And then Kathy had died.

A tumour had grown inside her brain in what

had been the most shocking diagnosis in all Verity's years of nursing. She remembered Jamie, white-faced and trembling, when he had called her into his office and told her that the prognosis was poor; remembered him breaking down in front of her, his face in his hands and his shoulders shaking with silent sobs.

It had taken Kathy two long years to die and Verity had seen something of Jamie's spirit die with her.

As a friend she had done what little she could. The most practical help she had been able to give them had to been to take Harriet out at weekends when Kathy was suffering the worst of her drug treatment. The chemotherapy had made her violently sick and all her hair had fallen out and Verity could have wept as she'd watched the once vibrantly beautiful woman slowly fade before their eyes.

But she had not been self-indulgent enough to let Kathy or Jamie see *her* grief; instead she concentrated on giving Harriet the best time possible, given the circumstances. Sammi and Harriet had become very close—the best of friends—and after Kathy's death Jamie had begun to include himself in the trips to zoo, the park and the cinema. Verity suspected that he'd found the outings as cathartic as his young daughter did.

And now, two years after his wife had died, Jamie had felt strong enough to take Harriet on holiday. One evening, after the four of them had shared a hamburger and the two girls had gone off to play, he had quietly asked Verity and Sammi to accompany them. 'Especially now you've got your passport!' he'd joked, but Verity had refused immediately.

'Why?' he had asked softly.

She'd said the first thing that had come into her head because she had not wanted to face her growing certainty that Jamie's feelings for her were changing. 'People will talk.'

He had smiled sadly. 'And do you care?' It had been one of those loaded questions, his eyes very intense as they'd watched her response.

'Of course I care,' Verity had answered lightly but she'd been aware that she'd been evading the real issue—of whether she cared enough about Jamie to begin a relationship with him and all that entailed.

The clock broke into her troubled thoughts as it rang out the half-hour, shrilly reminding her that if she didn't get a move on she would risk being late for work and she had enough on her plate to cope with without inviting a black mark from Sister Saunders! She might be best friends with the obstetric and gynaecological consultant but that didn't carry any weight where Sister was concerned and she was an absolute stickler for punctuality!

'Come here, Sammi.' Verity picked up a hair-brush from the mantelpiece, sat down on the sofa and pulled her daughter gently towards her, drawing her up to sit on her lap as she began to stroke the brush through the honey-coloured, silken curls.

Samantha wriggled impatiently, her dislike of having her riotous mop of hair combed well known, but Verity held her firmly. 'Please, darling,' she pleaded. 'Keep still for Mummy or I'll be late for work. It's nearly time to go to the childminder's.'

'Don't like the childminder's,' muttered Sammi sulkily.

Verity finished tying a blue bow with a flourish and leaned back to admire her handiwork. She knew that she was biased, but really——Sammi was the most beautiful child she had ever seen! 'She's a very nice childminder,' she corrected automatically. 'Of course you like her!' She frowned, the guilt she felt at having to leave Samantha every morning never far from the surface. 'She hasn't been horrible to you, has she, darling? Not Margaret?'

Samantha was honest, sometimes painfully so. 'No, Margaret's nice,' she agreed, as Verity heaved a sigh of relief. 'It's that William Browning!' she added indignantly. 'He always takes my biscuit!'

Verity bit back a smile. 'William's a boy, darling, and boys are different.' She wasn't sure whether this was a politically correct statement for a mother to make to her daughter but this morning, at least, she didn't care! 'Anyway, you're only there for an hour or so before you start school.'

'I wish *you* could take me to school!'

'And so do I, darling. So do I. But I have to earn the pennies to pay our keep, don't I?'

'I miss Harriet,' said Sammi suddenly. 'And Jamie.'

Verity swallowed one of her abiding fears. That Sammi was becoming too attached to the widowed consultant and his young daughter. And that things between her and Jamie were heading towards some kind of showdown. Like a coward, she put the thought away. She had quite enough to worry about at the moment without fretting about a situation which might never arise. She gave her daughter a tender smile.

'I miss them, too,' she said truthfully. 'There!' With a final flourish of the hairbrush the curls were tamed and Verity stood up and smiled. 'Now. Did I hear you say something about wanting cherries in your lunch-box?'

'Oh, Mummy—*can* I?'

Verity laughed. Pennies might be tight but she always made sure that they ate plenty of fresh fruit. She had added the cooled fruit to Samantha's packed lunch at breakfast-time. If only *she* could be so easily pacified by the thought of a handful of cherries for lunch! 'Sure you can,' she murmured indulgently, picking Samantha's blazer off the peg and helping her into it before grabbing her own jacket. She popped the umbrella under her arm for good measure—the recent late-April weather had certainly been living up to its reputation!

Then she clasped Samantha's small hand and set off for the childminder's more slowly than usual, subconsciously putting off the awful moment when she would have to walk into Theatre and come face to face with Benedict Jackson for the first time in almost six years.

The powerful E-type screeched to a halt in the staff-only car park, its British racing green colour glistening as the sun peeked out from behind a cloud to illuminate the droplets of rain which were spattered all over its distinctive bonnet. One long, long leg emerged from out of the low-slung door, followed by another, and then a spectacular example of muscle-packed male made a dramatic appearance as the driver of the car stood up to his full, impressive height of six feet three inches.

Benedict paused, his dark head turning a fraction as he was drawn to a movement on the other side of the car park, and his green eyes narrowed as he watched the girl running frantically up the steps towards the hospital entrance.

There was something very wild and free about her athletic movements, he thought. And something very appealing, too, about the yards of shapely thigh in their woollen tights which were fetchingly displayed by the short tartan skirt she wore.

He caught a glimpse of palest blonde hair peeping out from beneath a cute green velvet hat as the girl let her umbrella down and shook it vigorously and he stilled momentarily, his heart beating faster as some distant memory nudged disturbingly at his subconscious, but then the sun went in again and the memory was gone in an instant.

As he bent down to lock the car a uniformed

nurse strolled by, candid appreciation in her open smile, but Benedict scarcely noticed her. He had been used to women smiling at him like that since he was barely out of nappies! He was a man on whom the gods had chosen to confer more than their fair share of gifts and, consequently, he had never had to try too hard. Women came on to him strongly. Always had done. For years he had enjoyed the sensation—up to a point. But lately. . .

He sighed. What was it they said? About too much feasting making you long for famine! He had even tried famine recently—passing up every invitation which came his way. And invitations came thick and fast to Benedict Jackson.

So why was it that this jaded feeling, which clung to skin like grime, stubbornly refused to go away? Why did cynicism continue to harden his mouth into a tight, harsh line? Just what in hell did he need to put the spark back into his life? he wondered.

The hard mouth quirked as he watched the girl in tartan push open the glass doors of the entrance, her small, high bottom anatomical perfection as she wiggled off into the distance. Then he shook his head. There was more to life than a flounce of pale blonde hair and a flawless figure. Looking like that, he decided with chauvinistic pessimism, she would be bound to have an IQ in single figures.

Other men seemed to find their soul mates. So why not him?

He sighed again as he pocketed his car keys and made his way to Theatres.

*   *   *

'You're going to be late if you're not careful, Verity!' Sister Saunders was glaring as Verity tried to sneak past her office unnoticed but every nurse in Theatre knew that her bark was worse than her bite, just as they knew that she had a particularly soft spot for Verity or, more specifically, for Verity's daughter.

Verity nodded, pulling her wide mouth into an apologetic grimace as she slid to a halt. 'I know. Sorry, Sister. Sammi threw a tantrum when we got to the childminder's. And then, to cap it all, the seven-forty bus was cancelled.'

Sister Saunders's face softened, though not for very long. '*And* you're wet!' she accused. 'Though, quite frankly, Verity, if you wear skirts that short it's a small wonder you haven't always got double pneumonia! I don't know why you don't clad yourself out in something a bit more sensible!' she snorted. 'A pair of trousers and a thick sweater!'

'Yes, Sister,' answered Verity automatically, even managing a small grin. Her fashionable clothes were the one small rebellion left to her. When you got pregnant at twenty and the father had run off and become involved with someone else there wasn't really a lot of opportunity to rebel in other ways. Having a baby and a limited budget certainly put the kibosh on going out at night!

So she bought couture patterns and sewed them herself, knowing that her figure was good enough to get away with some pretty outrageous garments.

As hobbies went it was harmless and fairly non-addictive! And even though she *did* go out more often these days, with Jamie, she still kept sewing like crazy!

Her teeth chattered and Sister Saunders glared again. 'Now run away! Shoo! Get dry and get scrubbed up! I've put you in Theatre Two with the new boy. Jackson.'

Verity hurried along the corridor towards the nurses' changing room, the words clanging around inside her head. 'New boy'? She could almost have laughed aloud in different circumstances.

Benedict would be thirty now—three years older than her and hardly a boy. She had known him at twenty-four, when he was fresh out of med school. He had been no boy, then, either.

Infuriatingly, her heart thudded with the memory. Benedict Jackson had always seemed to be more of a man than any of the other new doctors. More of a man than anyone she had ever met, as it happened. Taller and tougher, his limbs more muscular and solid, his chin more prone to darken with stubble and much more experienced than the others. Oh, yes. Verity winced. Definitely more experienced. . .

'Whoa! Steady, Staff!' chided a voice, and Verity slid to a halt. She had almost collided with Ethel's sandwich trolley.

'Sorry, Ethel,' she said apologetically.

Ethel shook her head, although her tightly permed hair didn't move a bit! 'That's all right, love,' she said cheerfully. 'No harm done.' She hesitated. 'Did you know I'm booked to come in tomorrow, Staff?'

'What, for an operation?' asked Verity in surprise. Ethel had been working in Theatres for the last twenty years; she was like part of the furniture. 'I didn't know you'd been ill, Ethel.'

Ethel shrugged her plump shoulders beneath the flowery pinny she always wore. 'Not ill, really. Nothing to worry about, that's for sure!' She lowered her voice. 'I think it must be the change, Staff. You know. Periods coming more often than they should. Wretched things—as if I haven't already had enough problems with childbirth! I saw Mr Brennan in the clinic last week and he's booked me in for investigations. Pity he's away on holiday,' she sighed. 'I like Mr Brennan.'

'I'm sure Mr Jackson, the new senior registrar, is just as good,' said Verity immediately, smiling widely to put Ethel's mind at rest.

'You think so?' Ethel brightened up immediately.

'I *know* so,' said Verity firmly. 'I'd better go, Ethel, or Sister will have my guts for garters!'

'Want me to put you a sandwich aside?'

'Got any tuna and tomato?'

Ethel shook her head. 'Tuna and cucumber?'

'That'll do!'

'I'll leave it in the staff-room—you can pay me later!'

Verity went into the changing room, her thoughts ticking over. She hoped that Ethel's confidence wasn't misplaced. She knew that women of around fifty sometimes had changes to their menstrual cycle which they assumed to be simply the change of life—often not even bothering reporting it to their doctor. In fact, these changes were occasionally the symptoms of an underlying disease such as cancer.

Thank heavens that Ethel had enough sense to have been referred to Jamie, thought Verity, and mentally willed herself to stop fretting about it. Everyone knew that nurses—particularly theatre nurses—always looked on the black side of things!

She took off the damp tartan suit, the woollen tights and the ankle-boots and then slithered into the unisex pale blue cotton trousers with the matching short-sleeved top which all the theatre staff wore.

After she had locked her clothes away she hunted around in the wire mesh rack beneath the wooden bench until she located her own pair of white theatre clogs, with her initials boldly painted in black felt-tip on each cork heel! Verity had discovered within her first week of nursing that if you wanted to hang onto anything in the huge, impersonal surrounds of a hospital then it was best to personalise it!

She tucked the silken strands of her bobbed hair beneath the all-enveloping theatre cap and went to look at the operating list which was pinned up outside the changing room.

She quickly scanned it, relieved to see that the anaesthetist was Russell Warner who was slick enough and relaxed enough not to take nonsense from any new surgeon, however brilliant. And Verity was automatically assuming that Benedict would be in the élite ranks of brilliant surgeons.

The list was not what you might have described as uncomplicated but Verity was an experienced enough theatre nurse for it not to cause her any undue anxieties. Thank heavens! Apart from two routine sterilisations there was an anterior colporraphy—which was a vaginal operation for prolapse of the uterus, followed by a simple hysterectomy. If she was going to have to face Benedict then she wanted to be able to do it on automatic pilot. It was going to be difficult enough concentrating as it was, she knew, without having the added worry of a difficult and unusual procedure to cope with.

Though maybe he had changed, she thought, a touch hopefully. Maybe in the intervening years all that superbly honed muscle had slackened to a thick apron of fat around his abdomen. But Verity almost smiled as she brushed the thought away. Benedict Jackson *fat*? Instant world peace seemed a more likely scenario than *that*!

As she went into the instrument room to check that the night staff had laid out all the operating packs for that day's list she found herself wondering why she seemed almost relaxed about the thought of seeing him.

Almost. . .

Almost calm.

Perhaps because it all seemed so unreal. As though it wasn't happening. As though someone was going to turn around and tell her that it was all some big joke.

She picked out a pair of gloves and a gown then went to the trough-like sink which stood in an ante-room and began to scrub up, wetting her arms right up to the elbow and then covering them in vivid pink antiseptic soap and washing for three minutes exactly to ensure that they were properly clean.

A passing student nurse walked in with a cheery 'hello' and tied the back of Verity's pale blue gown.

When Verity was all gowned up she wandered into the instrument room where Anna Buchan was waiting for her. The second-year student nurse had only been working in Theatres for a fortnight but already Verity wondered how they had ever managed without her. She was a 'natural', with all the attributes needed by a good theatre nurse—manual dexterity, the ability to think on her feet and, most important of all, a non-panicky personality.

'Hi, Verity,' Anna smiled. 'I'm your "runner" for this morning's list.'

Which meant that Anna would assist Verity during the operation including, quite literally, 'running' around Theatre to add any extra instruments or sutures which the surgeon might require.

'My prayers must have been answered,' murmured Verity indulgently. 'Everything ready?'

'Yup!'

Verity wheeled her trolley into Theatre and opened the thick, green cloth to reveal the neatly packed silver-coloured instruments and packets of swabs and cotton wool.

'New surgeon, I understand?' remarked Anna conversationally.

Verity didn't lift her head, just carried on calmly separating and counting a packet of gauze swabs before laying them in a dish. 'So I believe,' she answered neutrally.

Fortunately, Anna was far more interested in her forthcoming wedding than in any new members of staff. 'Do you think I've lost weight?' she asked quite seriously and Verity *did* lift her head then— to grin.

'It beats me,' she answered, shaking her head in an exaggerated fashion, 'why brides-to-be always buy dresses too small, necessitating long weeks of working out in the gym and rigorous dieting so that they're exhausted by the time the big day comes. Poor things!'

Anna smiled and seemed about to say something, then appeared to change her mind and started adjusting the theatre light instead.

And Verity knew why. Knew that she was something of an oddity at work. Unmarried but with a child. People tended to make assumptions about women in her situation. Particularly men. And so she had developed a polite but somewhat brittle approachability where men were concerned. Even Jamie had never seen her with her guard completely down. She had made a fool of herself over a man once and had been hurt—badly—and she had no intention of allowing a similar situation to repeat itself.

Anna switched on the powerful, circular theatre light and the chatter of voices approaching told her that the rest of the operating team was assembling.

And then some second sense alerted her and she looked across the theatre to see Benedict walking into the scrub room from the corridor.

He was talking to Ted Lyons, his houseman, his deep, authoritative voice carrying into theatre. Verity bit her lip, listening in to what he was saying while she decided how best to greet him and expecting his voice to have changed. Or something.

But it hadn't. It was still deep and resonant with that sexy little chuckle that made it so irresistible.

'Hell of a journey,' he was saying. 'The motorway was down to one lane.'

'I noticed your car when you arrived,' said the houseman reverent. 'Top of the range, isn't it?'

'Uh-huh,' said Benedict rather dismissively and Verity felt like shouting a warning to Ted, who was young and ambitious and terribly eager to please. Except that he was going about it the wrong way with Benedict.

Don't be a sycophant, she felt like shouting! Don't revere him! I did all those things—mad, love-struck fool that I was. And he won't respect you if you do.

'So how does she handle?' the houseman quizzed.

'Like a dream,' answered Benedict slowly and

Verity knew without looking that his green eyes would have crinkled at the corners in the way that they always did when something gave him pleasure. . .

His voice took on a deep, distinctively intimate timbre as he talked about his car and Verity suddenly got a very good idea of what it must be like to be jealous of an inanimate heap of metal and chrome.

He had paused. She knew without looking up that he had seen her. That those green eyes would be interested and alert—his attention caught by the sight of an attractive young woman. Unless he had changed a great deal. . .

So, what to do? The mask concealed all but her eyes and if she kept those downcast then there was no reason in the world for him to realise that it was her. At least not for the moment.

Except that such behaviour would speak volumes, surely? Why go to the trouble of deliberately avoiding someone who meant absolutely nothing to her? And she was going to have to face him sooner or later. So why not be civilised about it? Cool, calm and collected, even? That's what all the agony aunts in the magazines would have advised her to do.

Cool, calm and collected, indeed! She felt none of those as Benedict walked across the operating theatre towards her, that elegant stance and impressive height and sheer breathtaking perfection dwarfing everything and everyone.

Hot, harassed and hounded would be a more

accurate description of her feelings—but she stood her ground. After all, *he* was the stranger here, not she. So, psychologically at least, she had all the advantages. *He* would be the one to be surprised by this meeting, not her.

He was almost upon her. Consciously she forced herself to relax, hoping that her body language would do her a favour and tell a pack of lies!

'Hi,' she said with cool politeness, looking up. 'You must be our new gynaecologist.'

He didn't answer immediately but then Benedict had never been one to conform to the conventional mores of behaviour. Instead he let his green eyes flick very casually over her from head to toe, not long enough to be offensive but just long enough to make her hormones heatedly shriek their recognition of this powerful, potent male.

'Yes, I am,' he replied. 'I'm Benedict Jackson.'

'I know.' She saw his eyes narrow. 'I saw your name on the off-duty,' she added, by way of an explanation.

He gave a slow, dizzying smile. 'Then I'm afraid that you have me at a disadvantage. You know who *I* am. . .' The dark brows were raised quizzically. 'But who are you?' he finished softly.

I'm the mother of your child! she nearly shouted hysterically into his face but some protective instinct stopped her. And what was the reason for that foolish hurt which had started plucking at her heartstrings like a rusty nail? Why on earth should he remember a brief affair which had taken place six years ago? Especially when she knew for a fact that she was merely one in a cast of hundreds who had starred in the fulfilling role of Benedict Jackson's bed-partner.

But even so she thanked some benevolent god that the theatre mask she wore hid most of the blush which stained her cheeks. And camouflaged the fact that she was biting her bottom lip hard enough to make it bleed. 'I'm your—' Verity swallowed and saw him hide a smile and it simply added fuel to her anger to realise the reason. He clearly thought that she was rendered speechless because he was so gorgeous! Oh, how she would like to pick up the nearest bowl of something cold and wet and sour-smelling and douse him with it! 'Scrub nurse,' she finished, on a gulp.

'Ah,' he murmured. 'And do you have a name, oh scrub nurse?' he finished, with gentle mockery lacing his voice.

It was now or never.

'It's Verity,' she answered tightly. 'Verity Summers.'

'Hello, Verity,' he said automatically, giving her a friendly nod, and had begun to turn towards his approaching houseman when he suddenly frowned and stilled.

She could see him racking through a mental computer printout of ex-conquests and if she hadn't been one of them she might have found it vaguely amusing. All the same, she didn't want to be standing in front of him when he finally remembered number one thousand and sixty or wherever she happened to be down the line!

'Excuse me,' she said and, sliding her right foot firmly back into her white clog, she began to move away from him.

'No, wait!' he instructed, still frowning. 'Verity?' he queried softly and his green eyes widened. '*Verity?*' He half stepped towards her but she raised her elbows in front of her chest to indicate that she was scrubbed, although the gesture was more one of keeping him away than of keeping sterile.

'Excuse me, Mr Jackson,' she said coldly. 'I've not yet finished preparing your instruments for the first case on the list.'

'Verity, I—'

'Are there any special instruments you prefer?'

He gave her a long, considering look. 'No,' he answered eventually.

'Glove size?' she queried crisply and saw the light of devilment in his eyes.

A light danced in his eyes. 'Can't you remember?' he murmured silkily.

'I never worked with you in Theatres!' she snapped back, furious at the sexual innuendo.

'That wasn't what I meant,' he laughed softly.

No. She knew exactly what he meant. Memory was a strange thing. And for years she had been able to remember every detail of his beautiful body and that included those wonderful hands, those long, strong and yet artistic fingers which could work such magic.

A huge wave of sadness engulfed her. If only he knew, she thought fleetingly. If only he knew that he had a beautiful five-year-old daughter sitting at her school-desk and learning her tables right at this very moment.

And he never would know! she vowed fervently. There was no way that she was going to let this no-good, philandering, flirting Casanova back into her or—far more importantly—Sammi's life. 'Glove size?' she repeated, in a tone of icy indifference and her attitude must have finally got through to him for he looked at her assessingly.

'Eight,' he answered, then added in an undertone meant for her ears only, 'And whose bed did you get out of on the wrong side this morning?'

'Certainly not yours!' she hissed with a foolish lack of thought or logic.

He shot her a look of pure sensual amusement. 'I can tell,' he purred, 'because if you had you'd be a lot less uptight than you are now.'

If she hadn't been scrubbed she really might have slapped his face. As it was she could see Ted, the houseman, coming over to talk to them so she contented herself—if contented could be the right word, given the circumstances—with a little yelp of impotent rage, accompanied by the most withering look that she could manage.

Then, and only then, did she move her sterile trolley to the back of the theatre to wait for the patient to be wheeled in, her tiny shudder seeming to indicate that she found his very presence contaminating.

CHAPTER TWO

THE first case was nothing more than a routine tubal sterilisation and certainly nothing to get into a tizz about but while Verity stood and waited, hoping against hope that she appeared calm and self-possessed, inside her heart was pounding fit to burst.

The sensation of unreality that had protected her like a cloak from thoughts of Benedict all morning and, indeed, all week had suddenly and brutally been whipped away, leaving her defenceless and vulnerable.

And though the *idea* of seeing Benedict again had caused her some disquiet, that was nothing to the cataclysmic effect of *actually* seeing him again. And while she had felt hurt because initially he had not recognised her and then felt indignant because he had flirted outrageously with her these feelings were nothing but trifles.

Because the over-riding and primitive feeling which had rocked her to the core was that on the other side of the room stood her child's father. As if that in some way bound him to her.

It didn't, she reminded herself.

And it took every ounce of self-possession she had to be able to stare calmly into a pair of flinty green eyes which were lit with what Verity considered to be wholly inappropriate appreciation as two nurses leapt to attention, almost fighting a duel to see which of them would be the lucky girl to tie the back of his blue gown!

Two seconds dragged by more than two hours would have done normally and Verity could have wept with delight when Russell Warner, the anaesthetist, brought in the twenty-two-year-old woman who was due to be sterilised.

Russell was handsome, in his late thirties and married to a fellow doctor—but this did not stop him flirting outrageously with any desirable female who came within a flirting radius!

This morning, however, a slight frown creased his brow as he connected the young woman to the tubes leading to the gases on the anaesthetic machine.

And Benedict had clearly noticed, too. 'Everything OK, Russell?' he enquired.

Russell gave a little shrugging movement. 'Nothing to worry about, I hope. She was a bit light when we first put her under so I've given her a little extra anaesthetic and, consequently, her heart rate has dropped a bit. Just give her a couple of seconds to adjust, would you, Benedict?'

'Sure,' Benedict nodded, and glanced over at the anaesthetic machine. 'So, what happened?'

Russell was watching the green blip of the electrocardiogram which was recording the patient's heart rate and it was a moment or two before he answered. 'Oh, she had a slight cough when they brought her up; I suspect that she has been smoking

on the quiet and didn't bother telling me about it.
For two pins I would have postponed the operation
and sent her back down to the ward but I gather—'
and here he raised his eyebrows above his mask
at Benedict '—that they had enough trouble getting her to have the operation in the first place.'

'That's right,' agreed Benedict in that distinctively low, lazy drawl. 'According to the notes. As
you know, Jamie Brennan saw her in the clinic
before he went on holiday.'

'Why on earth is she having a sterilisation at
twenty-two?' asked Verity with a frown. 'What
about children?'

'She has four already that she can't support,'
answered Benedict drily. 'This seems to be the
best solution in the circumstances.'

If it had been anyone other than Benedict, Verity
would have agreed with him. As it was she found
it impossible to consider his opinion impartially
and his words inflamed her, seeming to represent
male chauvinism at its very worst. 'Best for who?'
she demanded and saw Russell look slightly taken
aback. 'It takes two to make a baby, you know!
If her partner took some of the responsibility for
contraception then she would not be having her
fertility curtailed before she even reaches her mid-
twenties! But I suppose that being a man lets him
off the hook, does it?'

Benedict looked at her in surprise. 'Of course it
doesn't. And of course a man should be responsible for not bringing unwanted children into the
world. As it happens, this lady doesn't *have* a

partner,' Benedict pointed out. 'They've all been different.'

'Oh, *well*,' said Verity, 'if it's *morals* we're talking here—'

'It isn't!' Benedict retorted, a frown creasing his forehead as he observed her stormy reaction. 'As a matter of fact I agree with you—in theory. In practice, however—certainly in this particular case—it's unworkable.' He glanced across at Russell. 'Happy with her now?'

'Sure. Go ahead,' said Russell, smiling as he turned a dial on the anaesthestic machine. He certainly wasn't used to fireworks in the gynae theatre—not first thing on a Monday morning, anyway, and certainly not from Verity Summers who usually had the sunniest nature going!

Benedict cleaned the skin and frowned again as he held his gloved hand out towards Verity. Now what had *that* all been about, he wondered?

Verity handed him another swab, still seething but with herself rather than with Benedict. Talk about misdirected rage. If she was going to turn every case into a hidden agenda, attacking Benedict for having made her pregnant in the first place, then she might as well hand her notice in right now. Besides which, he *had* been responsible about contraception. Always. Even the very first time when, frankly, she had been so carried away that she wouldn't have cared whether he had used anything or not.

So it certainly wasn't *his* fault that it had failed to work. What was it they said? she thought

ruefully. That the only really safe method of contraception was total abstinence. Well, they
certainly hadn't practised *that*!

There was silence in the theatre, apart from the
puff and hiss of the ventilator which was 'breathing' for the patient, and the first case seemed over
almost before it had started.

The sterilisation had been done through a minute
incision in the umbilicus and it wasn't until they
brought the next case up—a hysterectomy that was
being done through the abdominal wall with all the
attendant risks—that Verity was able to properly
observe Benedict's operating technique.

Textbook surgeon; textbook surgery, she admitted to herself reluctantly as she watched his swift,
sure movements. The incision that he made in the
patient's abdomen was minute; you would barely
be able to see the scar when it healed, thought
Verity. Lucky were the women who had Benedict
performing a Caesarean section on them!

He was also one of those surgeons who talked
about the case while they were operating and
Verity admired that—it always seemed to make
the patient come alive for her. When a woman of
fifty was wheeled in to have an operation known as
a Marshall Marchetti—a procedure to cure stress
incontinence of urine—Benedict suddenly
announced, 'This lady used to dance at the
Windmill, wearing nothing but an elaborate dis-
play of scarlet feathers!'

And everyone burst out laughing, even Verity.
Because in Theatres—particularly for the

nurses, who only saw the patients when they were conscious for a few brief seconds——you ran the risk of becoming totally cut off from the human aspect of surgery. But Benedict, it appeared, was aware of this and compensated accordingly, chatting easily as he worked.

And this, too, served its own purpose. In Theatres there was always the potential for a 'life or death' situation. Experienced theatre staff always tended to keep the atmosphere as light as possible, except in real emergencies. Which was why a surgeon's reputation for talking about his golf game while exposing the abdominal cavity was often fact and not myth!

Verity gave a small nod of surprised approval as she observed him and then wondered why. After all, if he had *not* matured and become more rounded in the years since she had seen him then there would have been something very seriously wrong.

She had changed, so why not he?

It was just rather difficult, that was all, after years of thinking of him as the 'baddie' to acknowledge that he did have some good points. Although he must always have done, she chided herself, or else you wouldn't have fallen for him in the first place!

He deftly stitched through each of the four layers of the abdomen, his long fingers dextrous and his movements swift yet supremely steady.

How much easier it would be to dislike him, thought Verity guiltily, if he happened to be a duff surgeon! But when someone was *this* good then it was impossible not to admire them—from a professional point of view, at least.

She forced herself to act as if she was just another surgeon and to show him the same kind of courtesy. 'Is everything to your satisfaction, Mr Jackson?' she queried politely.

To his credit and her surprise he did not take the opportunity to make a wisecrack but merely said, 'Perfectly, thanks.'

But the list seemed to take forever. Verity watched the seconds ticking by on the large clock on the opposite wall in an effort to convince herself otherwise, wondering how it was possible that her whole perception of time had altered simply because Benedict was in Theatre with her.

Between each operation Benedict took off his gown and went through to the anaesthetic room to write in the notes before scrubbing up for the next op. Meanwhile Verity took her dirty instruments away, cleaned up and prepared her next set.

The procedure worked like an efficient and well-oiled piece of machinery. Patient after patient was wheeled in, operated on and then sent off to the recovery room prior to returning to her respective ward.

The last case was a little less straightforward than the others—a large ovarian cyst which had to be removed but which needed especially careful dissecting in order to save the ovary itself but which Benedict, naturally enough, managed without complication.

It was still only just past midday when they completed the list and Benedict tore his gloves off and threw them into the bin with an audible sigh of relief. No matter how simple and straightforward the first list in a new job was always slightly nerve-racking. You wanted—no, *needed*—to make a good impression. And that was generally—he didn't pretend to know what the form was for having your ex-lover standing across the table from you!

He looked into aquamarine eyes and suddenly his heart did a most uncharacteristic somersault. He smiled. 'Glad that's over,' he remarked conversationally and then couldn't help noticing that Verity had tensed up again, as she had tensed up on every occasion that morning whenever he had opened his mouth. What in hell's name was wrong with the woman?

The very masculine side of his nature considered the question literally. There was very little wrong from what he could see from here, which wasn't a lot. The loose pale blue top and trousers, which were visible now that she had removed her gown, certainly didn't show very much of her figure off. Mind you, he had always considered that style of pyjama suit was particularly unflattering; it made most women look like either stick insects or elephants, while Verity resembled neither.

No. She was a beguiling combination of long, athletic limbs and soft, gentle curves which were heaven to look at and heaven to touch. Now that much he *could* remember.

Suddenly it was all coming back to him—the brief, heady affair and the rather unsatisfactory conclusion to it.

His green eyes narrowed assessingly as he looked at her more closely. By the look of it she hadn't put on any weight in the intervening years. Except perhaps that her breasts were rounder; fuller. Mmm. Much fuller.

He felt a pulse beating a rapid tattoo at his temple and he abruptly turned away, unprepared for the excitement that flared up at the sudden memory of Verity's long, pale hair spread all over his pillow in the mess.

He went to wash up, shifting uncomfortably from clog to clog as he sought to alleviate the arousal that she had unwittingly provoked and deliberately dousing his wrists beneath an icy cold jet of water as he struggled to dampen down his thoughts.

Verity felt sick.

Violently sick.

White-faced and trembling, she slumped down onto the bench in the changing room and clutched her arms protectively around her stomach. Gisela Buxton, one of the senior staff nurses who had recently joined the staff, shot her a concerned look.

'Is everything OK, Verity?'

Verity opened her eyes and managed a thin smile. 'Everything's fine,' she lied. 'I'm just feeling a little queasy, that's all. It'll pass.'

Gisela, immediately jumping to conclusions as

was her wont, gave an understanding nod. 'That time of the month, is it? I'll go and make some tea for us, shall I?' She rattled on without waiting for an answer. 'That'll make you feel better! Come into the staff-room in a minute or two when it's ready. OK?'

Verity nodded, speechless with the irony of Gisela's words. That time of the month, indeed! The unwitting sentence brought back with chilling clarity just how frightened she had felt when she had discovered that she was pregnant with Benedict's baby.

She hadn't even need to do the test for confirmation. Her period, normally as regular as clockwork, had been over a month late but she had been so distressed by their break-up that she hadn't even noticed at first. Incredible to think about it now. She had told herself firmly that it was stress making her late but she had gone to the chemist and bought the kit anyway, meticulously following the instructions on the printed sheet.

Afterwards she had sat in the bathroom, staring hopefully at the test-tube as if hoping that science would confound her and deny what she knew in her heart to be true. . .

Lost in thought, she was startled by a knock on the changing-room door and, wearily, she rose to her feet to open it. There stood Benedict, as bold as brass, a remorseless smile curving that beautiful mouth.

'We'd better have lunch,' he said, without preamble, 'hadn't we?'

Verity mentally shook off the desire to agree with him, like a bull shaking off the matador's cloak. 'I'm not particularly hungry,' she answered repressively.

He looked at the set line of her mouth and the pale colour of her oval face, which made her eyes seem so startlingly bright, and nodded slowly. 'No,' he agreed. 'Perhaps not. Some coffee, then?'

She didn't know what to say. Perhaps honesty was the best policy. She turned candid aquamarine eyes up to him. 'Why bother?'

He looked slightly taken aback as if he wasn't used to having his wishes questioned.

And perhaps he wasn't, thought Verity. She had certainly never raised any objections to anything that he had suggested to her during the few heady weeks of their affair.

'Isn't it obvious?' he asked. 'Why I want to speak to you?'

She sighed. 'Of course it's obvious but don't worry, Benedict,' she told him indifferently, 'I'm not intending to cramp your style while you're here.'

He frowned. 'That wasn't what I meant.'

'Wasn't it?' she challenged coolly.

'No.' Then he said, in quite a different tone altogether, 'You've had your hair cut.' It was the first time that he had seen her without the theatre cap and he could now appreciate how the pale, heavy hair hung in a silken curve to her jaw. It suited her; made her look much more sophisticated than the waist-length tresses she had sported all those years ago.

And Verity replied, before she could stop the stupid, petty, give-away words, 'So you *do* remember.'

A touch of irritation hardened the corners of his mouth. 'Of course I remember! We——'

Verity shook her head. Oh, no. Not that. Please not that. She couldn't bear him to tell lies; to make what had happened between them into something that it wasn't. 'We had a brief fling, yes, Benedict. Nothing more than that. It was nice while it lasted but I really can't see any point in hashing over it.'

He gave a bemused smile but the unmistakable irritation lingered on. 'Do you give *all* your ex-lovers such a hard time, Verity?'

Oh, how he would laugh if he realised that he was the only man on whom that unique honour had been conferred. Verity tried a different tack, amazed at this sudden flowering of hitherto unknown acting ability. 'They aren't normally quite so persistent,' she chided gently.

By way of response his clever, slanting green eyes immediately swivelled to her left hand, as though seeking the only logical reason why she should be so off with him!

His glance took in the ringless fingers and he found that he was disproportionately pleased. 'You aren't married?' he queried, barely able to keep the smile from his lips.

She was so tempted to lie. After all, the reason she wasn't wearing a wedding band could be explained away by the fact that rings were often cumbersome when you were constantly washing your hands all day. Lots of nurses didn't bother to wear them for that very reason. But somehow, staring straight into those perceptive green eyes, Verity found it impossible to lie to him and she heard herself saying aloud, 'No, I'm not married.'

Was she imagining the glint of satisfaction in his eyes that greeted this throw-away statement or was her ego simply manufacturing it in a pathetic attempt to save her hurt feelings because it had taken him so long to recognise her?

'So why won't you have a cup of coffee——?'

But at that moment Gisela Buxton's approaching voice thankfully saved the day. 'I've made a pot of tea, Verity!' she called, and there was the sound of a door swinging closed, accompanying her words, before Gisela appeared. 'Come and—— oh!' She stopped in mid-sentence as she saw the tall, dark figure of the new senior registrar standing at the open door of the nurses' changing room. 'Hello, Mr Jackson!' she said cheerfully, curiosity burning brightly in her eyes.

Benedict nodded. 'Gisela,' he acknowledged pleasantly, with a smile. 'Was that tea I heard you mention?'

'It certainly was!' Her eagerness knew no bounds. 'Would you like a cup?'

'I'd love one,' he agreed blandly, his eyes meeting Verity's in gentle amusement though she took care not to react to his conspiratorial smile.

Gisela beamed. 'Come on, then. It's in the staff-room—freshly made, too! And you, Verity!'

Verity's heart sank. Short of making a scene, there seemed little else to do than to follow Gisela into the staff-room, with Benedict close on her heels.

And all the time Verity's mind was working overtime, wondering whether anyone would be perceptive enough to make the connection between Benedict and Sammi. Including the man himself. Everyone knew that she had a child, yes. But that was all they knew. Even to Jamie she had only sketched what information she had deemed was absolutely necessary. And all that she had told those who were brave enough to ask her was that things had not worked out between her and Sammi's father. Which was, of course, absolutely true.

The staff-room was empty, although perhaps that wasn't surprising as the lists in the other theatres had obviously not finished yet but, there again, Benedict had proved to be an exceptionally speedy surgeon.

On the centre table stood a pot of tea with all the accoutrements laid out and next to it sat a pile of ready-wrapped sandwiches, left there by Ethel.

'Great,' smiled Benedict, and settled himself down on one of the chairs, stretching his long legs in front of him in an attitude of relaxation and crinkling his green eyes appreciatively at Gisela. 'I'm absolutely *starving*!'

Gisela, a happily married woman in her forties, was still young enough to respond kittenishly to

Benedict's undeniable charm and immediately took over the role of hostess. 'Did you buy anything from Ethel, our sandwich lady?'

Benedict shook his head.

'Then, here,' Gisela said busily, handing him one of the packages. 'Have this—it hasn't got a name on it! These tuna and cucumber are absolutely delicious—and you look as though you could do with a bit of feeding up!'

'Thanks.' He unwrapped the sandwich and bit into one half with a healthy appetite, while Verity sat down on the chair furthest from him.

'How do you like your tea, Mr Jackson?' fussed Gisela.

'Benedict,' he corrected roguishly. 'Milk, no sugar. Fairly weak. Thanks.' He finished chewing and raised a dark eyebrow in Verity's direction. 'Not eating, Verity?'

She wasn't about to tell him that he was wolfing her sandwich down! She gave a faint smile and shook her head.

'Verity isn't feeling very well,' explained Gisela, as though she wasn't in the room with them.

'Oh?' There was the twitch of a smile. 'Nothing catching, I hope?'

Verity knotted her fingers together in her lap. 'I hope not,' she told him, with toneless insincerity. Why wouldn't he let up? Just leave her alone? He always had had the confidence and ego of a colossus—which in itself wasn't surprising, given the man's physical and intellectual gifts. Was this, she wondered, all intended to pander to that ego? Embarrassing ex-girlfriends by resurrecting shameless, toe-tingling memories best left forgotten? And doing it by simply lifting a corner of that oh-so-sensual mouth?

Though the irony was that she had far more of Benedict's than some mind-bending memories of trips in sports cars, followed by sumptuous dinners and then seemingly endless nights of bliss in his tiny room in the doctors' mess.

He was the biological father of her child.

And perhaps. . . The thought dogged her like a persistent itch as she watched him demolish the last mouthful of her sandwich. Perhaps it was Benedict's right to know about that.

She took her cup of black tea from Gisela and sipped it, more for something to do with her hands than because she really wanted it, her heart pounding as she considered her options.

If she told him there was no predicting what his reaction might be and her life and, more importantly, Sammi's life would never be the same again.

But if she didn't tell him. . .was that morally right? The question gnawed away uncomfortably at her conscience. Six years on the answer did not seem so clear-cut as it had done before; there were complicated shades of grey now where, in the past, there had only been black and white.

Whatever the case it was not something to be decided on the spur of the moment, especially not with the man in question sitting opposite her with

his jade-green eyes fixed on her with that disturbingly speculative, smoky gaze.

And whether she told him about Sammi or not—
was there really any point in antagonising him just
because once he had hurt her? Whatever happened
she still had to work with the man. She had
responsibilities—namely a child to support. She
couldn't allow herself the luxury of just flouncing
out of Theatre and out of his life. However tempting the prospect might be. . .

Forcing what she hoped was a pleasant smile,
she sipped at her tea. 'So, what made you decide
to take the job at St Jude's?' she queried.

Benedict gave a small smile, as if amused by
this sudden reversion to bland hospital chit-chat.
'I admire Jamie Brennan and the work he's been
doing on infertility.'

'Oh. Yes.' With a shock, Verity realised that she
had scarcely given Jamie a thought all morning.

'He's read some of my papers,' said Benedict,
his green eyes lighting up with enthusiasm. 'And
he seems to like them. He's even prepared to let
me do some clinical trials here. . .' His voice
trailed away as he became lost in thought, his mind
skipping to the paper that he had just finished
writing.

It had been the devil of a piece to get down just
the way he had wanted it and there had been a
good deal of midnight oil burnt in the process. But
he had heard yesterday morning that it had been
accepted by the *British Journal of Obstetrics and
Gynaecology*. He smiled unexpectedly.

Verity blinked. She had forgotten just how mesmerising that smile could be. 'So that's the reason you're here?' she queried.

Benedict looked surprised. 'Isn't that enough? As London hospitals go it has an excellent reputation,' he shrugged.

'And so does St Thomas's.' Her voice sounded accusing.

He fixed her with that emerald stare, the smile still playing around the corners of his mouth. 'That's true. But why should I go there?'

'Because you trained there! Because your family built half the wretched hospital!' answered Verity hotly, completely forgetting about not antagonising him. 'And donated half the wards! I should have thought that would have guaranteed you an open-armed welcome *there*!'

As opposed to here, she might almost have added. Benedict's smile increased; it was not the first time today that she had shown the passionate, tempestuous side of her character which had been so in evidence during their brief but heady affair. 'Ah,' he said softly, deliberately echoing her earlier words, 'so you *do* remember?'

'Of course I remem. . .' But Verity's words tailed off awkwardly as she noticed Gisela looking from one to the other of them, now almost bursting with curiosity.

'Do you two *know* each other?' she demanded.

'No!'

'Yes!'

Verity and Benedict spoke at exactly the same

time, only fuelling Gisela's confusion. The time had come, thought Verity grimly, to nip any speculation in the bud. Her aquamarine eyes glittered a warning to Benedict as she spoke. 'Yes, we knew each other,' she said lightly. 'Vaguely. We trained at the same hospital, didn't we, Benedict?'

His eyes glittered.

'Along with about five thousand others!' went on Verity sarcastically, all the anger that she had repressed spilling out in her words. 'Heavens,' and she exaggeratedly rolled her eyes upwards, 'it must be getting on for five years now, mustn't it?'

Suddenly it was no longer funny. Benedict's eyes narrowed at Verity's deliberate mistake. Why the hell did she seem to dislike him so much? A muscle worked in his cheek. 'Nearly six years, actually,' he corrected, his bland words at odds with the distinct flash of irritation in his eyes.

He's angry that I can't pin it down to the exact time and date, the arrogant so-and-so, guessed Verity with wry amusement. 'Is it really that long?' she queried, with false surprise. 'Goodness! Doesn't time fly when you're having fun?'

'Doesn't it?' he agreed mockingly.

Gisela had started to fidget uncomfortably. She wasn't the world's most perceptive person, thought Verity, but quite frankly you would need to be made of stone not to have picked up on the atmosphere between her and Benedict. You could have cut it with a knife!

Gisela rose to her feet. 'I must go and make a phone call,' she said awkwardly.

'Thanks for the tea,' murmured Benedict, and was rewarded with a blushing smile.

'You're welcome!' gushed Gisela, her embarrassment forgotten and, with a rather mystified glance in Verity's direction, she scuttled off.

Her anger vanished and, feeling rather deflated and foolish, Verity took the opportunity to stand up as well but so, infuriatingly, did Benedict.

'It's time I was going,' she told him.

'Nonsense,' he demurred softly, with a glance down at the discreetly expensive timepiece that gleamed against the hair-roughened skin of his wrist. 'We have at least twenty minutes before we're due back. Why don't we take the lift down; get some fresh air?'

Verity shook her head so that the gleaming blonde bob shimmered in a silvery-pale haze. 'I never leave the theatre suite during my lunch hour.'

'So make an exception.'

Oh, the *arrogance* of the man! When would he get it into his thick skull that she simply wasn't interested? 'Just for you?' she queried.

'Mmm. Just for me,' he said, his eyes crinkling with silent laughter, and Verity felt a great wave of regret for how things might have been. If only he had cared for her as much as she had cared for him. . .

'Why should I?' she challenged.

'Because you want to?' he suggested.

'I don't,' she told him frostily, and as she went to turn away he murmured her name with an intimate and blatantly sensual undertone which only an ex-lover could have got away with.

'Verity? Don't you realise?' he quizzed softly. 'That if your intention is truly to keep me at arm's length then you're going entirely the wrong way about it.'

Her blue eyes widened in genuine confusion. 'And what's that supposed to mean?'

He shrugged the broad shoulders, clad in their thin covering of blue cotton that did little to conceal the solid muscle beneath. 'Just that, like most men, I find a challenge a terrific turn-on. All the thrill of the chase. So trying to distance me has entirely the opposite effect. Was that your intention?'

'No, it certainly was not my intention!' Verity shot back, and she felt the hysteria that had been simmering away all morning begin to bubble up inexorably towards the surface. 'And you're not to talk to me like that! You're not! You don't have the right!'

'Don't I?' he queried insolently. 'Doesn't the fact that I was once your lover give me any rights at all?'

'No, it damned well doesn't!' Verity declared furiously. 'You were the one who was about to leave for another hospital without even bothering to tell me. Or do you have a defective memory?'

He gave her a careless smile. 'As I recall we had a row, a fairly spectacular row, and said a lot of things in anger. . . In fact, *you* were the one who walked out, Verity.'

'I had no choice in the circumstances,' she retorted coldly.

'Maybe not,' he conceded slowly. Because he could have stopped her; could have gone after her and she would have come back to him in a moment. But he hadn't. He had been young. Glad for an excuse to end a relationship which had been getting way too serious for a newly qualified doctor. It hadn't been until later that he'd realised what he had lost and by then it had been too late to make amends. Like an ice-cream left out in the sun to melt, Benedict had allowed his relationship with Verity to spoil.

He pushed his long fingers back through the thick, dark hair and this gesture vividly reminded Verity of how he used to look first thing in the morning. And that hurt, too.

'But just because,' he added, giving her a shrewdly assessingly look as if daring her to deny the attraction between them that still fizzled beneath the surface, 'it didn't work out then it doesn't mean we couldn't give it another go, does it? Hmm? We were both much younger then.'

Verity couldn't believe that she was hearing this, she really couldn't! In fact, she was so shocked that even though she had opened her mouth to snap back a reply she found herself, quite literally, unable to speak.

Benedict's gaze was steady. He noted her reaction first with interest and then with intense curiosity. There was something in her behaviour

that puzzled him but he was damned if he could put
his finger on it. He had bumped into ex-girlfriends
before, many times, but none of them had ever
shown him quite so much hostility. Quite the contrary, in fact. But, conversely, neither could he
remember feeling so overwhelmingly attracted by
an ex-girlfriend as he was by Verity. The years
had made her even more beautiful, if that was
possible.

'But even if you aren't interested in me as a
man any more, Verity,' he persisted, 'does it have
to be quite so fraught at work? We *are* colleagues,
after all, with nearly six years' maturity under our
belts. We don't have to engage in a slanging match
every time we meet, surely, just because we once
had a fairly tempestuous affair? Aren't we a little
more civilised than that?'

He elevated his eyebrows quizzically and Verity
almost fainted with shock, stunned senseless
by the recognition of a hauntingly familiar
expression. She swallowed. Sammi didn't look
like her father, no. She was all fair where he was
dark, soft and rounded where he was hard and
lean. But that play of features that she had just
witnessed. . . Verity realised that she had just seen
her daughter mirrored in Benedict Jackson's face.

And a cold chill broke out on her skin as she
realised that what had happened in the past was of
little consequence now.

Benedict *did* have a right but that right had
nothing to do with being her ex-lover. The right
he had was blood-borne and powerful and it over-

rode everything else. *He was Sammi's natural father!*

And, sooner or later, she was going to have to tell him. . .

CHAPTER THREE

BENEDICT frowned. Their spat temporarily forgotten, he put an instinctive hand out towards Verity. For one moment there he had been convinced that she was about to go and faint on him. What on earth had he said? he wondered with genuine alarm and confusion. She looked as though she had just seen a ghost!

'Are you OK?' he queried solicitously, and then nodded with memory. 'Of course! Gisela said you weren't feeling very well—please sit down. Let me fetch you a glass of water—'

'No!' Verity's words rang out as clear as a bell. Her mind was made up. She would have to go through with it—she *must*! For Sammi's sake more than Benedict's. For didn't her daughter have a right, too, to begin to know her father? And the sooner the better. 'Benedict—' she began huskily, when the door opened and a whole bevy of theatre nurses walked in, chatting away merrily.

Something in her voice stilled him. 'What?'

She shook her blonde head impatiently, casting a frustrated look at the blue-clothed women who had seated themselves at the next table and were casting curious looks in their direction. 'It's nothing,' she said, then shook her head again as he frowned. 'I mean— Oh, heck! Listen, come round to my flat—'

For a moment he thought that he must have misheard, in view of everything which had gone before. '*What?*' he queried incredulously.

'Come round to my flat,' she repeated, aware that the nurses on the next table were almost falling off their chairs trying to listen in to their conversation. She shook her head. 'I'll talk to you about it later,' she said abruptly and headed for the door but Benedict moved as swiftly and as gracefully as a panther and he stayed her with one strong hand resting loosely around her tiny wrist.

'When?' he asked immediately.

The room had lapsed into silence. The nurses sat agog, self-consciously pretending to eat their sandwiches. Verity distractedly shook his hand off. For heaven's sake! she thought despairingly. He may not care about his own reputation—but he might have the decency to consider hers! She marched out of the staff-room and he followed her along the corridor until she was forced to stop and stare into those green eyes which, even against her will, she still found so mesmerising.

'When?' he persisted, a slight urgency deepening his voice as though he was thinking that he might have imagined her invitation.

When indeed? Verity gave an inward sigh. Why put it off? The longer she worked with him and the more she grew used to him as a colleague then the harder it would be to tell him. 'Tonight.'

He gave an exaggerated grimace. 'Tonight isn't good,' he told her. 'I'm on call.'

Verity suppressed a sigh. No, it wasn't good. But the alternative was another day of existing in this highly unsatisfactory limbo while her imagination ran riot wondering just how Benedict would greet her momentous news. And what if someone else told him that she had a child? What if clever Benedict Jackson managed to work it out for himself? She wouldn't put it past him. What then?

She pulled her narrow shoulders back, her resolution strengthened. 'I don't live that far from the hospital,' she informed him. 'You could be back here in minutes if there was an emergency—it would take you about the same time as from the mess.' Then she wished to high heaven that she hadn't mentioned the mess, with all its associations.

'Tonight it is, then,' he agreed in a murmur, his voice still edged with surprise.

Verity saw the instinctive light of desire which lit his eyes from within and bile rose up in her stomach. She swallowed, almost changing her mind, but some deep and instinctive need to tell him urged her on from within. 'Oh, don't get your hopes up, Benedict,' she advised cuttingly. 'It isn't what you're thinking.'

He didn't bat an eyelid. A woman hadn't spoken to him this way in years; he was rather enjoying it. 'And what am I thinking, Verity?'

'That we're going to pick up where we left off!'

she accused bluntly. 'And we all know where that was!'

He hadn't been, actually. He had been thinking the very opposite, wishing that he had given himself more time to get to know her before. That the physical thing between them had not been so swamping and that they had not fallen into bed within hours of meeting one another. Somehow, with the benefit of maturity, he suspected that Verity Summers had hidden depths that he hadn't even been close to tapping.

'Why don't we meet tomorrow night instead?' he suggested with a smile. 'I'm not on call then and we could have dinner together. There must be some superb restaurants round here.'

Verity sucked in a breath. To tell him in the neutral setting of a restaurant might be better. But even if she had wanted to have dinner with him, it was impossible. Tomorrow was Tuesday and the woman who lived downstairs and who babysat when Verity was on call was at college on Tuesday nights. And she would never get another trustworthy babysitter at such short notice, not in the city. But she didn't want to start on the subject of childcare difficulties because that would prompt all kinds of questions.

And although Verity knew that by the end of today she would face being interrogated by Benedict she didn't think that she could handle it now. Not at work, where she might dissolve into tears and make a complete fool of herself. And, besides, she didn't even *want* to have dinner with

him. She shook her head. 'I'd rather speak to you
tonight,' she said.

'What time?' he asked calmly.

'About nine?' she managed, with an air of quiet
self-possession that almost matched his. At nine
he would already have eaten and Sammi would be
safely tucked up in bed. Surely that would be the
best way?

'OK. Tell me where you live.'

She recited her address and he nodded—not
bothering to write it down, she noticed.

Benedict gave a smile that didn't quite meet his
eyes and nodded. 'Until later, then,' he said, and
headed off in the direction of the lift.

Verity watched him go in silence, realising that
his words hadn't been entirely accurate.

She still had an afternoon's operating to get
through before she was able to confront him with
the truth. . .

By the time the list had finished Verity was bushed.
Benedict came up behind her as she was discarding
her blood-stained pale blue gown, the tension of
the last operation draining from his face by the
second. He had opened up a forty-year-old woman
who had presented with vague symptoms of
abdominal discomfort to discover that she had car-
cinoma of the ovary—and that the disease had
spread, her body so riddled with it that Benedict
had had no choice but to close the patient's
abdomen up again.

The appalled atmosphere in Theatre as he had

silently sutured had been almost palpable, everyone present realising with horror that this relatively young mother of three would be dead before the year was out.

And during that operation Verity had never worked so instinctively with a surgeon before, not even Jamie—she had seemed to anticipate what Benedict needed almost before he realised himself. It had made her think, too, her own problems suddenly seeming terribly insignificant when compared with what lay ahead of the patient on the table.

As he approached, Benedict suddenly saw the long, slender line of Verity's neck and he felt his pulse quicken. 'Hi!' he said softly.

She turned around, suddenly embarrassed, realising that whatever tenuous camaraderie existed between them at present it would not survive tonight's heart-to-heart. 'Hi,' she said quietly.

'Thanks for your help back there.'

She shook her head. 'It was just—'

'No,' he interrupted, with a smile, the most genuine smile she had seen all day. 'It wasn't "just" anything. That was a pig of an operation.'

'Those types always are,' she observed with quiet perception.

'I know.' He hesitated, wanting to say something nice to her—something that might stop her looking either angry or fearful when she saw him. He suddenly found that he wanted to make that wide, soft mouth curve into the kind of welcoming smile he remembered so well. 'You're a superb scrub nurse, Verity.'

And stupidly she blushed, the compliment mentally demolishing her. It meant too much; that was the trouble. A few words of professional appreciation somehow implied a respect that had never been there when she'd been nothing more than his willing bed-partner. 'Th-thanks,' she stumbled, then let herself relax enough to smile. 'A good surgeon makes it so much easier,' she told him honestly.

The smile dazzled him; started his heart beating in a way it hadn't beaten for years. 'Listen,' he said huskily, 'are you quite sure you won't change your mind about having dinner with me?'

And she was tempted, so terribly tempted. If they had just met she wouldn't have given the question a moment's hesitation. But, then, if they had just met she wouldn't have invited him round to her flat like that. And probably given him entirely the wrong idea. . . 'No, thanks.'

Not bothering to pursue it, he said, 'Do you have a car?'

She shook her head and laughed. 'On a nurse's salary? You must be kidding!'

'Then at least let me drive you home. It's still raining.'

'I have an umbrella——'

'I know.'

She raised her eyebrows questioningly.

'I saw you arrive this morning.' His voice deepened with appreciation. 'In a tartan suit. With a matching green velvet cap. You looked—superb.'

'I was soaking wet,' she answered disbelievingly.

'Mmm,' he agreed, the corners of his green eyes
crinkling, 'I know.'

He had somehow managed to make getting wet
sound like the ultimate in sensuality. Another compliment. It made her realise how emotionally
barren she must have become if these small words
of praise could have her warming like a schoolgirl.

'So, shall I pick you up outside in, say—' he
glanced at his watch '—twenty minutes?'

Verity shook her head. 'I told you—it isn't far
from the hospital.' Which was true. What he did
not know was that she always had to go to and
from work via the circuitous route to the childminder's—to collect Sammi. It was just her luck that
the only childminder who measured up to Verity's
exacting standards lived in the opposite direction
to the hospital. The journey was a pain but she
would rather have a pain of a journey and the peace
of mind that came from knowing that her daughter
was in the best possible hands.

Verity glanced down at her watch and realised
what the time actually was and gave a squeak. 'No,
thanks,' she told him breathlessly. 'I have to. . .go
to the supermarket on the way home.' She could
see that he was about to offer to drive her there,
too, and so she gave him a brief smile, said,
'Excuse me,' and headed off to the changing room,
thinking that he was much harder to cope with
when he was being nice to her.

It turned into one of those days. The bus was late and Sammi was sulking by the time she picked her up from the childminder's. Consequently she dragged her heels going home and by the time Verity pushed the front door open the two of them were very wet and very disgruntled.

The normal evening routine of cartoons, tea, playtime, bath and story did not follow their usual fairly smooth progress.

Time marched on and every time that Verity tried to hurry Sammi along the child responded by slowing her pace right down.

'Darling, please eat your carrots!'

'I don't want them.'

'Your peas, then.'

'Don't want them, either!'

'There'll be no pudding if you don't eat some vegetables!' said Verity automatically and Sammi completely overreacted by having a tantrum, sending her fork spinning across the kitchen table.

'Anyway!' she sobbed loudly. 'You're not eating *your* supper, Mummy!'

'I don't feel like eating,' answered Verity quietly, so edgy about Benedict's visit that she actually felt nauseous.

'And neither do I!' shrieked Sammi, the tantrum growing in volume. Which made two in one day, thought Verity wearily, as she gave in without a fight and cleared away the plates before going to run a bath.

But even bathtime failed to work its usual magic or perhaps Sammi was simply too tired to enjoy what was left of the day. Verity seemed to end up wetter than her daughter and didn't even attempt to wash the butter-coloured mop of curls, just battled to get Sammi into her nightie and helped her brush her teeth.

She read aloud the story of Pigling Bland but Sammi heard it through, still determinedly wide-eyed by the end of it so that Verity was forced to wade through *Jemima Puddleduck* before her daughter began to look even remotely sleepy. It wasn't until she had reached the end of the *Tale of the Pie* and *The Patty-Pan* that Sammi's eyelids drifted down to cover her eyes and she dozed off into a fitful sleep.

Verity sat on the edge of the bed for a moment or two, just watching her.

Strange how, since meeting up with Benedict again today, she could see the facial similarities between the two of them so clearly. The lack of likeness between father and daughter was only superficial, Verity realised with a rapidly beating heart. OK, so Sammi might be blonde and blue-eyed where Benedict had dark hair and eyes of jade but that determined little jut of the lower lip, the strong squareness of the chin. . .

Oh, the similarities were there all right, if you cared to look for them. . . It was just that in the past there had seemed no point and Verity had firmly pushed them to the back of her mind.

The loud ring of the doorbell startled her and she glanced at her wrist in horror to see that it was nine o'clock already and that Benedict was

prompter than she remembered. But, then, she
had been so cloyingly eager before that she
would probably not have murmured a word if
he had turned up an hour late for a date!

But it's not a date, she reminded herself as she
snapped on the night-light, her skin going cold as
she realised what a state she had left the flat in in
her battle to get Sammi to bed.

Oh, dear Lord! The tea-things were still on the
table and there were toys all over the sitting-room
floor. And she hadn't even emptied the bath-tub.

She glanced in the mirror. Add to that her ruffled
hair and the old jeans and shirt she had changed
into—now all crumpled after the bathtime exer-
tions—and she hardly exuded the quiet air of calm
needed to impart her momentous news.

The doorbell rang again; there wasn't even
going to be time to scoop up some of the plastic
toys that lay scattered around haphazardly all over
the hideously patterned carpet.

Verity walked towards the front door, feeling
irritated. She was by nature a tidy person and first
impressions counted. Benedict would look around
then sum her up as a slob. And she was no slob.

But you aren't trying to *impress* him, are
you? taunted an inner voice. Leastways, you
shouldn't be.

She pulled the door open to find him on the
doorstep, his arms full of packages, the green eyes
all crinkling up at the corners and droplets of rain
glinting off the dark, ruffled hair.

'Hi!' He held out a bag of macadamia nuts,

a box of Belgian chocolates and a foil-wrapped package of coffee so good that Verity could smell it from where she stood.

She took the packages awkwardly, disarmed by his thoughtfulness and making the prospect of what she was about to tell him all the more difficult. 'Oh. Thanks. You shouldn't have bothered to bring anything.'

'On the contrary. You refused my invitation to dinner and as I'm on call I couldn't bring wine. This was the least I could do. Unless, of course,' he added teasingly, 'you aren't going to invite me in?'

'I'm sorry.' She held the door open, holding her breath and waiting to hear his first words as he walked into her home. Somehow they were terribly important to her.

At least he didn't break into a flood of false compliments—that would have been just too much. The flat was small and cheaply furnished but it was all she could afford. And although tonight it looked like a pigsty underneath the debris it was fundamentally clean and she hoped against hope that Benedict would realise that.

She heard his inrush of breath as he registered the toys.

He turned round to face her, shocked. 'You have a child?' he demanded.

Straight to the point, at least. 'Yes, I have a child.'

'But you told me you weren't married!'

She almost smiled. 'I'm not married,' she answered gently. 'It isn't mandatory.'

'No.' He was clearly having trouble imagining her as a mother. 'So there's no husband?'

She shook her head. 'No. No husband. Sammi's father didn't—marry me.'

Something niggled at him. Something that wasn't quite right. Verity a mother! She looked too young, too slim, too damned innocent! He struggled to find something neutral to say. 'And how old is your daughter?' he asked politely. 'Sammi—wasn't it?'

Still clutching the goodies he had given her, Verity realised that there was going to be no easy way to do this. No right time to tell him. Why bother settling him down with his coffee and his nuts and his fine chocolates? Would that somehow lessen the blow?

'She's five,' she told him, her voice sounding oddly calm.

He nodded. 'That's a nice age,' he murmured dutifully, desperately searching around for the kind of remarks that his married sisters always seemed to make about other people's children. 'Bit of a handful, I expect?'

And then he froze.

It wasn't just the time span; it was the measured way that she had told him—the slightly diffident expression in her eyes as she waited for his reaction.

He narrowed his eyes and stared at her from beneath dark, suspicious brows.

Verity prayed for strength. 'Benedict. . .' she began, but her words tailed off hopelessly.

The twist of his mouth became ugly. 'Just what are you trying to say, Verity?' he demanded harshly.

She hadn't rehearsed it; it came out in a tumbled rush. Perhaps that was the only way that it could have come out. 'That you are. . . That Sammi is. . . She's your daughter,' she finished huskily.

The words seemed to spill into his mind like cold, hard pebbles. He felt strangely powerless, as though the gods had decided to play poker with his future. And there stood Verity, her beautiful face pale and calm and her icy blue eyes steady, as though she had not just dropped into his lap the unwelcome news that he was the father of her child.

Or was he?

His mouth twisted as his eyes scanned the room as if searching for something and then he seemed to find it for he strode over to the mantelpiece above the mock-coal fire and picked up the framed photograph that stood there.

His eyes raked over it. He found himself looking at a stranger. A stranger, moreover, with floppy curls of honey-coloured hair and eyes as blue as a hyacinth. If someone had asked him to sit down and draw his imagined child's portrait then this fair little girl, with her soft pink and white complexion, would be its very antithesis. His relief and his anger knew no bounds. With a trembling hand he replaced the photo, then turned on Verity.

'Is this your idea of a joke?' he demanded furiously, and he noticed almost dispassionately that his hands were still shaking. 'What or who in the hell do you think I am, Verity? Some kind of patsy? A willing sucker? Do I *look* like the kind of man who would just calmly accept paternity from someone he hadn't seen in years? Someone, moreover—' he paused deliberately; the chance to wound her just too tempting to resist '—with whom he had had nothing more than a brief affair?

'Or maybe—' and his green eyes glittered '—maybe I'm not the only lover you've confronted like this. Will anyone do? Perhaps,' he suggested cruelly, 'you've worked your way down a long list before you finally reached me.'

The implication behind his words was shocking—that she had entertained a whole series of men in her bed. Verity trembled violently and the packages in her hands slid unnoticed to the ground as he continued to storm at her.

'What were you hoping for?' he demanded harshly. 'Some kind of financial support?' His eyes slid around the untidy room with contempt. 'You sure look as though you could use some!' And somehow her passivity enraged him even further.

'Let me give you a tip, shall I, Verity. Hmm? That the next time you attempt to entrap a man you ought to go about it with a little bit more finesse. At least tidy up a bit! Soft lights and music are the traditional accompaniments to such ploys, you know—not showing a man into a pigsty where you couldn't even be bothered to clear away your supper plates! Being a slattern doesn't have a *great* deal to commend it!'

The anger continued to flare over him like an all-consuming flame. He wouldn't let up. He *couldn't* let up.

He was caught in the blue light of her startled eyes but let his gaze sweep downwards, disparagingly taking in her crumpled clothes. He could hardly believe that this was the same woman he had seen from the car park this morning, who had worn that outrageously fashionable tartan miniskirt with the matching jacket and the jaunty green velvet cap.

His voice was as hard as stone. 'Jeans may look sexy but they aren't very practical for seduction. I assume that that *was* what you had in mind, was it, Verity?' He paused to draw breath, the blood thundering furiously in his ears, when his bleeper shrilled loudly in his ears and the sound brought him back to his senses. Barely able to bring himself to look at her, he shot out a terse question, 'Where's the phone?'

'Over there.' She pointed to the phone, which had been chosen by Sammi and which was fashioned in the shape of Donald Duck.

But as Benedict picked up the receiver, punched out the number and began speaking into the bilious yellow beak not a glimmer of a smile appeared on his lips.

'Mr Jackson here,' he bit out, and there was a tense, awkward silence while he listened.

'What's her blood pressure like now?' he

demanded, and nodded his head while he listened. Even in her distress, Verity could tell by the look on his face that whatever the case was it was, indeed, very serious.

'I'm on my way,' he said curtly and put the receiver down, drawing a deep breath as he sought to control his breathing and to calm himself down enough to safely get into a car and drive it. And, then, to perform an emergency Caesarean on a woman who·had gone into premature labour.

The midwives were worried about her: there was protein in her urine; she was oedematous, which meant that she was retaining fluid in her tissues, and her blood pressure was now danger-ously high. These three signs meant that she was imminently in danger of having what was termed as a pre-eclamptic fit. And both mother and baby were at risk.

He stared at Verity as though he had only just seen her for the first time and his mouth tightened with distaste.

'I'm needed on the labour ward.' Still she said nothing and still he felt the urge to lash out at her as he moved swiftly towards the door. 'If you think that I have a case to answer; if you persist in accusing me of fathering your child—'

'"Accusing"?' she blurted out in dismay. *Had* there been accusation in her words to him? She had thought that she had told him gently and with-out blame or recrimination. She felt indignant and, with her indignation, a little of her normal spirit returned. 'I wasn't *accusing* you of anything, Benedict!'

He gave her a cold, hard look, as if she hadn't spoken. 'If you persist with your claim,' he repeated softly, 'then you'll have to prove it in a court of law!' and, turning on his heel, he opened the door and walked straight out of the flat and Verity despised herself for feeling grateful that at least he hadn't slammed it and woken up his daughter.

CHAPTER FOUR

As soon as Benedict had gone off to deal with his emergency in Theatre Verity began moving around the flat, bending to pick up the toys from the floor and then putting the larger ones in the big, plastic box that stood hidden behind the sofa. Trying not to see how it all looked through his eyes. Cramped and untidy—a pigsty. He had actually said that himself.

And trying not to dwell on how he saw *her*—a broke, single mother desperate enough to try anything to try to foist paternal responsibility onto him.

She began to straighten up all the pieces of furniture in Sammi's doll's house—something that she hadn't done for a long time. It was tedious but satisfying for the small girl in the morning and useful in its way to Verity herself. Because if she kept busy, she kept telling herself fiercely, then she wouldn't have time to think; to dwell on Benedict's appalling reaction to the news that he was her child's father.

After the toys had been cleared away she picked up the coffee and chocolates which he had brought—still lying on the ground where she had dropped them—and carried them through into the kitchen, where she stuffed them angrily into the

70

store cupboard. Then she filled the sink with water and began washing up almost, she thought rather grimly, as though she was trying to punish herself in some obscure way. Because washing up she normally hated but tonight she almost welcomed the dreaded chore.

It took her a good hour and a half to clean the place to her satisfaction and she went about it rather obsessively, wiping down all the cupboards with lemon-smelling cleanser and even polishing the pine kitchen table with wax so that by the time she had finished the small flat was gleaming.

Verity looked around and gave a small nod of approval. If Benedict could see it now he wouldn't be so jolly critical, she thought proudly, and then her knees buckled and threatened to give way and she sat down abruptly in the nearest chair and began to cry.

It wasn't a loud crying session. She didn't dare; she certainly didn't want to wake Sammi. Instead the tears just slid silently down her pale cheeks; kept on coming and coming until there were no tears left to cry and it was only then that she rose to her feet, washed her face and blew her nose, brushed her hair and made a strong cup of tea.

She was tempted to put a drop of whisky in it but it would only guarantee that she woke in the morning with a headache, and *that* she could do without. Besides, the alcohol might dull her senses and she needed all her senses about her while she worked out what to do next.

She should not have told him—it was as simple as that.

And whether or not she had been influenced by a soft heart and a guilty conscience that made no difference at all. She had not thought it through properly before she'd blurted it all out to Benedict. And if she was being perfectly honest just what had she *expected* his reaction to be?

That he would embrace without question a five-year-old child as his own? Start taking her to the zoo on Saturdays and the park on Sundays?

Verity put her cup down on the table with a trembling hand. And he had said. . .had said. . .

That had been so hurtful—the way he had implied that he was simply one in a long line of lovers.

But. . .

Had she not done the same to him? Assumed that *he* had had hundreds of other women?

When the stark reality was that neither of them really knew *anything* about the other. Their affair had been of the short, sweet, passionate variety—although the ending had been inevitably bitter. Verity sighed. It seemed such a long time ago, as though it had happened to a different person.

They had met at a disco at the doctors' mess—hardly the most thrilling location in the world! Verity's set of nurses had that morning received the results of their nursing examinations. Verity had passed! A whole group of them had decided to go to the disco.

Verity had been dancing with a couple of her

friends, not exactly boogying around her handbag but pretty close to it!

But she was in a devil-may-care mood and having the time of her life. She had drunk no more than a glass of wine but that had been on an empty stomach on what was her first night off after a week of night duty on a very heavy geriatric ward. Some of the patients had been extremely sick and some of them terribly lonely and frightened.

It had been a depressing week, the most depressing since her nursing career had begun two years previously, and maybe that was what had made Verity throw caution to the wind. That night she had suddenly felt like celebrating her youth and vitality and good health. She had never been to a party in the mess before; the rumours that she had heard about their wildness had put her off!

An only child, Verity had been brought up strictly by extremely old-fashioned parents. They had been delighted at her choice of nursing for a career but reluctant to let her leave home at just eighteen. But there had been no alternative to moving away because there was no local hospital where she could have done her nurse training and continued to live at home.

Verity's family doctor had been influential; he could see that, given the opportunity, Verity's parents would allow her no personal freedom at all. It had been he who had encouraged her to try for the biggest and the best of the London training hospitals, even though it was a good distance from the quiet village where she had grown up.

Which was how Verity had ended up at St Thomas's, thrilled and yet rather daunted by training at a hospital with such a high-powered international reputation!

But her fears had proved groundless; she had adapted to the hard, physical work and additional study of anatomy and physiology like a duck to water. And she had warily steered clear of any social functions, preferring to study or to take advantage of the city's galleries and become a 'culture vulture'.

Until that night.

Being more the jeans and T-shirt type, Verity had borrowed a dress from one of the other nurses. Short, shiny and silver, it had been the last thing that she would have chosen normally. Though maybe that might all change in the future, she'd though as she'd given a twirl in front of the full-length mirror in her room.

She had not been a vain girl but even she could not fail to see that the silver dress had looked an absolute knockout, with her long, pale blonde hair flowing freely down her back. She had been acutely aware that she had never been stared at by the opposite sex quite so much as when she'd walked into the darkened room, where the flashing coloured lights and the loud, throbbing music had made it seem like a different world. But no one had caught her eye.

Until she'd noticed that every woman on the dance floor seemed to be gravitating towards one corner of the room.

And then she'd seen why and had swallowed.

He had been standing there grinning, drinking a glass of beer and surrounded by members of both sexes who had all been vying for his attention, as courtiers would a king. He was, in the most corny way imaginable, very tall and very dark and *very*, very handsome. Astonishingly so. Verity had likened it to going out to buy some paste earrings and being tempted by the most costly diamonds.

There was no point.

So she'd turned away and given herself back to the sway of the music, not knowing that Benedict had observed the movement with interest, experienced enough to realise that she was not being intentionally provocative and yet he'd still been young enough to have known an almost unbearable, swamping desire that had driven every other thought from his mind, bar the one that had said he must have her.

For no woman had ever subjected Benedict Jackson to a cool once-over and then turned her back on him.

Benedict was an instinctive master where women were concerned. Where other men might have gone straight up to her or tried to catch her eye he did neither. He carried on listening, sometimes talking, and only occasionally did he let his gaze drift to the supple, shimmering beauty with the hair like pale moonlight all the way down her slender back.

And of course, Verity, even with all her inexperience, soon became acutely aware that her eyes seemed to be having some kind of dark, tingling two-way conversation with the best-looking man in the room.

So by the time that he *did* actually come up to her, smiled that devastatingly careless smile and said, 'You look much too hot to dance any more—come and have a drink with me,' Verity was in no mood to resist. She let him buy her a drink and introduce her to all his friends and it took for ever before slow music succeeded the frantic throb and he was able to pull her into his arms and bury his head in the fragrance of her lovely hair as he had been longing to do all evening.

Benedict resisted the strongest sexual urge that he had ever had and made no attempt to seduce her that night, arranging—most uncharacteristically for him—to see her the very next evening.

But a sleepless night for both of them and the sultry heat of summer, adding to a torment which neither had experienced before, conspired against them and Verity had ended up in Benedict's bed, unable to resist the inner storm which raged and convinced that she had fallen in love with him.

For the first time in his life Benedict felt out of his depth. Before, lovers had been one very pleasant part of a very pleasant life and he had enjoyed his love affairs immensely. But something about Verity was different. He found that he felt an almost ugly, primitive need to stamp his domination on her. He wanted to make love to her constantly and they rarely left his room in the mess.

Consequently, his work suffered and Benedict

was an intensely ambitious young man. In his more unreasonable moments he blamed Verity and the spell she had cast on him, which he seemed powerless to resist. Benedict found himself in a situation where he was not completely in control and mentally, if not physically, he tried to retreat.

And while all his inner turmoil had been taking place, Verity had been given a 'friendly' warning by another nurse that Benedict was infamous for being the 'love 'em and leave 'em' type. She was petrified that it was going to happen to her, too, and she began to question him when he was late, convinced that he had started to see someone else. She would confront him and they would row and the row would end up passionately in bed but each spat somehow diminished the relationship as a whole.

The news that he was leaving St Thomas's came to Verity like a thunderbolt out of the blue. The same nurse who had warned her of his reputation took it upon herself to say slyly, 'I suppose you've heard? Benedict's landed the surgical rotation at the Manchester General!'

Verity nearly choked on her coffee. *Manchester?* But that was *miles* away!

The nurse must have registered the shock and the hurt on Verity's face but it didn't stop her. 'Don't say he hasn't bothered to *tell* you he's going, Verity?'

No, thought Verity with a grim, numb ache. He hadn't bothered to tell her.

He had given her a key to his room and so Verity

was waiting for him, white-faced and trembling, when he came off duty.

Benedict had been up all the previous two nights assisting in emergency operations. He had then had to work his normal long days on the wards. He had seen a girl of nine die, had not slept in almost forty hours and felt almost ill with fatigue. He saw the accusation in her eyes and gave a silent groan. A ding-dong with Verity was just about the last thing he needed right now.

'Why didn't you tell me you were leaving?' she demanded as soon as he had closed the door behind him, her hands on her hips like a fishwife.

Not even a kiss, he noted sourly. Or the opportunity to lose himself in the magic of her embrace. He sighed, took a can of cola from the fridge and drank from it before answering. 'You must have known that I was coming to the end of my house jobs,' he pointed out, wondering why he was evading her question. Just why *hadn't* he discussed moving hospitals with her? Was it because his obsession with Verity Summers was becoming like a thorn in his side?

'Why didn't you *tell* me?' exploded Verity furiously, with far more vehemence than she had intended. She rubbed her temple abstractedly; it was odd how up and down she had been of late— not like her normal self at all.

Benedict repressed a yawn. What he needed above everything else was sleep. Comforting, restorative sleep—and lots of it. What he did *not* need was an endless tirade of clichéd accusations.

'Verity, sweetheart,' he shrugged, 'I need to go to bed—'

She misinterpreted his words completely. 'I'll bet you do!' she shot out wildly. 'That seems to be all you ever *do* want to do, doesn't it! Making hay while the sun shines; is that it, Benedict? Is *that* why you didn't tell me you were leaving? Have you got another eager and willing lover lined up for you at your next hospital?'

His temper snapped and he said the unspeakable. 'Not yet,' he drawled and put the half-drunk can of cola down on the table. 'I plan to exercise a little more discretion next time around—I'm steering clear of women who feel that they have some God-given right to interrogate me as if we're *married*, or something—'

Verity didn't stop to think. She picked up the can of cola and hurled it at his head.

With the instincts of a survivor and a sportsman, Benedict ducked. The can hit the wall and exploded in a spray of brown, sticky foam, most of it gushing over Verity but some spotting Benedict's white coat. The absurdity of the situation made him burst out laughing. He was about to take her into his arms to kiss her and then to maybe lick a few of those sweet drops of cola from that long, smooth neck of hers. . .

But Verity heard nothing but the mocking laughter; registered little but the fact that he was going away and that he hadn't even bothered to tell her. 'I *hate* you, Benedict Jackson!' she screamed, and there was an angry thumping on the wall from the occupant of the room next door.

Desire died. Benedict's mouth twisted with scorn, fatigue and anger. 'Keep your voice down,' he told her cuttingly. '*You* may have got your obligatory eight hours last night but a great many of us didn't. Including me. And now, if you don't mind, Verity, I'm really very tired. . .'

She took one last, lingering look at him, her heart breaking into tiny pieces and her pride all she had left—urging her to be the one to end it. 'And I am very tired of this relationship,' she returned shakily. 'That's if you could have ever called it a relationship. Somehow I doubt it.'

She allowed herself one final look into those flinty green eyes and then she walked out of his room, not even bothering to shut the door behind her. . .

The shrill ringing of the doorbell broke into her tortured memories and Verity started, to discover that it was two in the morning and that she had been sitting and staring into space for hours, raking over memories which were probably best left forgotten. As she came to, she sniffed with surprise as she looked around at the remarkably spotless flat, remembering the scene before Benedict's bleeper had taken him tearing back to the hospital.

The doorbell rang again.

Just a brief, sharp and short ring, but it could be no one else but him. She rose to her feet as reluctantly as a heavily pregnant woman and pulled the door open.

She was shocked at Benedict's appearance. His face was ashen, his hair a mess and the green of his eyes was almost completely obscured by the hardened jet of his glittering pupils. Poignantly, there was a drop of bright red blood above one eyebrow which had obviously splashed there while he had been operating. There was no warmth in the green eyes when they looked at her.

'I want to see her,' he said.

'You can't. She's asleep.'

'I want to see her,' he repeated obstinately.

Verity sighed. She had neighbours on both sides and it was two in the morning. 'You'd better come in.'

But she couldn't help but notice the way that he almost flinched from the contact as her arm brushed briefly against his, as though she repulsed him. Though maybe she did—and who could blame him? Did she have the right to have kept his child a secret from him for all these years?

He stood in the centre of her tiny sitting room, dark and brooding and thoroughly dominating. 'Where is she?' he demanded, looking around the room as if expecting to find Sammi tucked up on the sofa.

'Benedict,' she told him in a soft, protective voice, 'Sammi is sound asleep and she has school in the morning. If she is woken up in the middle of the night by a total. . .' She bit her lip and her words tailed off as she realised just what she had been about to say so tactlessly. And truthfully.

'Stranger?' he supplied acidly, and then his

mouth curved with scorn. 'I may be a novice where children are concerned, Verity, but I'm not *completely* stupid. I don't intend to wake her up and frighten her. I—just—want—to—see—her.' He emphasised every word of his final sentence as though he was talking in a foreign language.

It was a bald entreaty which Verity could not ignore. In fact, its very starkness gave her a brief sensation of comfort. Better that he cared and was bitter than not to care at all. Verity nodded. 'Very well.' She gestured with her head. 'Come with me.'

Sammi's tiny bedroom was off a short corridor which led from the sitting room. Verity pushed the door open and went soundlessly inside, her heart in her mouth, aware of Benedict just behind her.

The bedroom was, at least, something that she could be proud of. Sammi had just graduated from popular Disney characters to girly-girly toys and Verity had decorated the room in just about every permutation of pink that she could think of! She bent over to check that Sammi was sleeping, twitched the duvet unnecessarily and then rather reluctantly moved away to allow Benedict to approach the bed.

He stood there for some time, not moving—so silent that Verity could not even hear the sound of his breathing as he watched the steady rise and fall of Sammi's chest.

Something prompted her—some instinct, Verity could not have said what it was—to leave him there alone with Sammi and she retreated noiselessly from the room, going straight into the kitchen where she made a pot of strong coffee, though she used her own brand and not the stuff that he had brought with him. Then she took it into the sitting room and waited.

In the bedroom Benedict stared down at the little girl with something approaching awe. He was used to dealing with new-born babies or, very occasionally, his nephews and nieces.

But this was different.

She was. . . He almost trembled with emotion as recognition stirred deep within his soul.

She was *his*.

She looked so small and so very perfect. He stared at the pink and white bloom of her skin which was illuminated by the soft glow of the night-light. At the dark blonde lashes that brushed in perfect half-moons against her chubby, childish cheeks. At the tumble of golden, mussed curls which lay in silken coils over her pillow. And something dug at his heart as again he remembered how her mother's hair had used to lie like that.

For it never occurred to Benedict to ask himself whether Verity might be lying. He knew without doubt and without question that he was Sammi's father.

Abruptly he left the sleeping child and walked blindly back into the sitting room, his eyes focusing to find Verity perched on the edge of the sofa with a tray of coffee steaming on the small table in front of her.

How pale she looked, he thought dispassionately—her aquamarine eyes bruised by shadows and the pale blonde bob badly in need of brushing. She still wore the old jeans and crumpled shirt that he had been so critical of earlier, though the bathtime splashes had naturally dried by now. And yet she must have known that he would return.

Stupidly, her obvious neglect of her appearance touched him far more than the stirring of desire that he had felt for her in Theatre earlier that day, in what now seemed like a lifetime ago.

When was the last time he had been in the company of a woman who had not spent her whole time preening herself? The women he dated wore clothes that probably would have cost what Verity earned in a single month at the hospital. How the hell did she *manage* to bring up a child on her meagre wages? he wondered, with sudden savagery. Were her parents helping her out?

'W-would you like some coffee?' asked Verity nervously as she recognised the renewed anger in his eyes, not sure whether he would storm out or insult her again or what.

The incongruousness of the polite question brought a brief quirk to the corners of his mouth but then the reality of the situation hit him like a blow to the solar plexus. What the hell was he going to *do* about it? He met her questioning stare and brought himself back to the present with difficulty.

'Thank you.' He nodded his dark head formally. 'I could use some coffee.'

'You—you've got blood on your forehead,' she

told him distractedly. 'It looks like arterial,' she added, though she couldn't for the life of her have said why.

Benedict walked over to the mirror that hung above the mantelpiece and frowned. So he had. His mouth tightened as the sight of the blood brought the horror of the case he had just operated on after rushing back. He had been in Theatre within minutes of leaving Verity's house, to find that a Caesarean section was not just preferable but essential.

Benedict sighed. There were attendant risks to all surgical interventions and a Caesarean was no exception. The hazards of this particular operation were those of anaesthesia, particularly aspiration of vomit in the unprepared patient. Also haemmorrhage at the time of operation and, immediately following it, thrombosis or embolism which could occur—deadly clots which could lodge in a woman's veins and halt circulation of blood flow to the main vessels of the body. Causing death.

Advanced maternal age meant that the dangers were accentuated and the patient that Benedict had operated on was thirty-five.

By the time that Benedict had pulled the baby boy free he was flat, registering 0 on the Apgar scale which assessed a new-born's condition. The tiny infant was pale blue due to lack of oxygen, had limp muscle tone and his heart rate was absent. They had managed to get him breathing again and he was now lying in a cot in the special care baby unit under the care of the neonatal paediatrician and hanging onto life by a thread.

Every second that he survived now counted considerably. He might make it until the morning with a bit of luck or help from the Almighty—depending on whether or not you believed in a God. Benedict had met very few surgeons who did.

Meanwhile, the baby's mother was being nursed in the intensive care unit.

Benedict rubbed ineffectually at the spot of blood, emerging from his thoughts to see concerned aquamarine eyes set in a pale face staring at him in the mirror with concern.

'Do you mind if I wash?' he asked brusquely.

'Of course not,' Verity answered quickly, sensing his inner distress. It must have been some emergency, she thought. 'The bathroom is next door to Sammi's room—'

'Thanks,' he said shortly. 'I'll find it.'

She heard the sounds of taps being run. It sounded strangely and falsely intimate—to have a man in her bathroom like that. Her hand shook suddenly with the irony that it should be Benedict in there. The only man she had ever been intimate with. . . Sad, really, that she should never have recovered emotionally from a relationship which had clearly been so one-sided.

The sound of running water stopped and she watched him walk slowly back into the room. He had obviously dampened his hair down, too, and then run his fingers through it in the absence of a comb or brush. He had always done that, she remembered with a pang. His hair had usually been mussed if he was called in the middle of the night when they were in bed.

He used to stumble around, trying to get dressed in the dark, until she would murmur and tell him that she was awake anyway and she would lie back on her pillows watching him slick the dark waves into some semblance of order.

Because she would stay awake for him, no matter how tired she was or how long he took to operate. So that when Benedict came back to bed it was always to her open arms and soft kisses.

Benedict saw the wide-eyed way she was looking at him and he remembered, too. But remembering was a big mistake, the erotic yet sharp pull of lust momentarily distracting him. And distraction was the last thing he needed in this bizarre situation, which was quite new to him.

Hell's fire, he thought distractedly as pure feeling and the need for comfort flooded through his veins and he forgot all else other than how good it had felt to have Verity so soft and compliant in his arms all those years ago. And remembering suddenly, too, how she had always waited for him to finish a case, no matter how late. How he had always made love to her on his return and how easily she had soothed his troubled mind and body. He found himself longing for that incomparable release right now.

He shifted uncomfortably in an effort to dispel the yearning and moved to sit on a chair on the opposite side of the room to Verity, who was trying very hard to act as though nothing was untoward.

'How do you like your coffee?' she enquired. 'Still black, with sugar?'

'The very same.' He gave her a look of wry surprise.

She silently poured him a cup and handed it to him, then sat back and sipped her own coffee and waited for him to speak.

But Benedict didn't speak. He drank his coffee in the hope that it might get rid of the fatigue and the confusion but it didn't. He felt the dull ache of hunger in his stomach and realised that he had had nothing since his sandwich in Theatre at lunchtime.

Verity recognised his dazed look for what it was. Emotionally and physically the man was overloaded. 'Have you eaten, Benedict?' she asked softly.

'Not unless you count the sandwiches that Gisela gave me.'

Hell, that was hours ago. She rose to her feet. 'I'll get you something.'

He didn't attempt to dissuade her. He was pleased to have her out of the room, to be alone with thoughts that were whirling around in his head like clothes in a spin-drier.

Verity bustled around in the kitchen for something quick, easy and filling to give him.

In ten minutes she returned, carrying in a tray of fresh pasta with a basil-flecked tomato sauce topped with Parmesan shavings and an accompanying side dish of salad. Fragrant on a side plate sat a hunk of warmed Ciabatta bread.

Benedict almost drooled and took the tray from her with a grateful smile, the burden of their undiscussed daughter forgotten as his body went into survival mode and demanded the food that it craved.

He ate quickly, thought Verity, like all surgeons on call who had no idea when they might get the chance to eat again. When he had finished every mouthful and wiped the last trace of sauce off his plate with his bread, Verity went back into the kitchen to make more coffee. They were sure as hell going to need it.

She washed up while she waited for the kettle to boil and when she carried the tray next door she almost dropped it in surprise for Benedict was sprawled along her sofa, long legs hanging over the edge and his eyes closed, sleeping the sleep of the exhausted.

In sleep there was much more of the man she remembered. His lashes curved in two symmetrical charcoal arcs on his cheeks. The cynical lines had relaxed; he looked young and quite, quite. . . Verity swallowed back the salt taste of what felt suspiciously like tears. . . Quite beautiful, she decided, the wistful expression on her face betraying the ache that she felt in her heart.

She hesitated, knowing that she should wake him and yet reluctant to cut short the sleep that he so obviously needed.

'Benedict,' she whispered softly.

'Mmm,' he murmured into the cushion and, moving his body one hundred and eighty degrees, he turned to face the other way, nestling as he did so and sliding his hip ever deeper into the sofa.

Compassion won out over common sense and Verity went over to the sleeping man. I'll take his shoes and socks off, she decided, and if he sleeps through that then he deserves to sleep.

She removed both, shocked by her desire to run her fingertips over his bare feet, then went to fetch a blanket from the store cupboard and tucked it around his sleeping frame as tenderly as she would a patient.

I'll set my alarm for six, she thought as she snapped the light out. That way he can be out of here before Sammi even wakes up.

She allowed herself one last, lingering look. 'Goodnight Benedict,' she murmured softly but he could not hear her.

CHAPTER FIVE

BENEDICT woke to find himself in a hard, unfamiliar bed and he stiffened, his senses on full alert until he realised that it was not a bed and that there was no woman next to him. And then he wondered if he was going completely mad because he had not been involved with a woman for well over a year. Almost two, actually.

No. He was on a sofa. Verity's sofa.

He looked down and blinked, wiggling his toes experimentally. His feet were bare and someone—obviously Verity herself, since he doubted that Sammi had got up in the middle of the night!—had covered him up with a blanket.

He felt in need of a bath, a shave and a coffee, in that order. He felt like hell but at least he had slept the night through.

He lifted his wrist up into the air and narrowed his eyes to see that it was almost six o'clock and then he became aware of a small figure standing in the sitting-room doorway.

She looked like a child from a story-book—all pink and clean in her nightdress, a battered teddy-bear dangling from one hand. She looked at him fearlessly, direct as only a child could be.

'Who're you?' she asked, as though she was

used to seeing strange men asleep in her flat every day of the week.

Was she? he wondered savagely.

'Are you a friend of Mummy's?'

Yes, he thought grimly, I suppose you *could* say that. Something that went far deeper than sense and decorum prompted Benedict to sit up and lean forward to hold his hands out to the small girl. And, amazingly, she came and took them, looking into his green eyes with frank interest, and Benedict knew that he could never lie to this sweet innocent. So please don't ask me again, he prayed. Not yet.

'Are you?' she persisted. 'A friend of Mummy's?'

'Y-yes,' he answered, but he couldn't help himself from sounding doubtful. Put like that, it made him seem as though he was one in a cast of thousands. And Sammi was clearly unconvinced, too.

'Why are you sleeping on our sofa?' she demanded.

'Because I was tired.'

The simple logic of this seemed to appeal to the child. 'Mummy doesn't let Jamie sleep on the sofa,' she objected. 'And *he's* a friend.'

Benedict felt his skin turn to ice. Jamie? Jamie who? Not Jamie *Brennan*, for heaven's sake? Don't say that Verity was involved with his consultant!

'So you must be a very special friend?' Sammi persisted.

It was the mention of Jamie Brennan that did it;

that activated Benedict's response. And the response came from somewhere deep inside him—some fundamental layer of himself that he had never before explored. 'I'm your father,' he heard himself telling her.

There was a loud gasp and instinctively his hands tightened protectively around Sammi's but the sound had not come from the child but from the pale-faced figure at the door where Verity stood, watching and listening, stark horror written all over her delicate features.

She looked so fragile, Benedict thought. The belt of some filmy, flowery dressing-gown thing was tightly tied around her slender waist. As though if you touched her she might snap.

Verity stared at Benedict with cold, condemning eyes, literally shaking with rage. How could he? How *could* he?

Sammi, seeing her mother and sensing the suddenly hostile atmosphere, ran over to Verity to be picked up and given a huge cuddle, Verity's eyes sending out messages of silent fury towards Benedict.

'Mummy—that man says he's my daddy!' Oh, Mummy! *Is* he?' And as Verity looked down into her daughter's face and saw a million childhood fantasies blossom into magnificent life she did not have the heart to do anything other than nod in agreement. She would deal with Benedict later.

But how was she going to explain to Sammi? She gave her daughter a final kiss, then put her back down. 'Darling,' she smiled, 'go and get your uniform on, would you?'

'Mummy, do I *have* to go to school?'

'Yes, you do,' came a firm, deep voice from across the room and Benedict walked forward, the green eyes glinting with a humour which Sammi clearly found irresistible. 'Just as Mummy and I have to go to work.'

Sammi cocked her blonde head to one side. 'Do you work with Mummy?' she asked interestedly.

'I do now. I just joined the staff yesterday.'

'Are you a—doctor?' asked Sammi tentatively.

'Yes,' he smiled.

'What kind of doctor?'

She had never asked Jamie that, thought Verity suddenly. Not once.

'An obstetrician,' replied Benedict. 'And a gynaecologist. You see—you get two for the price of one!'

'What's a—a—'strician?' faltered Sammi.

'I look after women who are having babies, that's the obstetrician bit,' he explained. 'And I help them have their babies—that's the gynaecologist bit.'

'Oh.' Sammi's face crumpled. 'Have you got lots of children like me, then?'

Verity thought her heart would break in two when she heard the desolation in that little voice. And she found that she, too, was regarding him watchfully, holding her breath as she waited to hear what his answer would be.

He sensed the expectancy as he shook his dark

head. He found it easier to meet Sammi's eyes than Verity's. 'No, Sammi,' he answered quietly, and then he did allow himself to meet that aquamarine gaze. 'You're the only child I have in the world.' He might have added a bitter and accusatory 'to my knowledge' if he had been alone with Verity. He might have done a lot of things if he had been alone with Verity.

But he wasn't.

Verity sensed his tension, aware of all kinds of unspoken messages sizzling between the two of them. She cleared her throat, suddenly nervous. 'Please go and get dressed, darling,' she prompted. 'And then we'll have breakfast together. How's that?'

Sammi looked up, unable to hide the eagerness in her voice. 'Is *he* having breakfast with us?'

'No!' Verity's voice was determined.

'Yes!' Benedict's sounded softly confident.

As had happened in Theatre yesterday their conflicting messages were relayed at exactly the same time and Sammi blinked in confusion as she looked from one to the other in much the same way as Gisela had.

Verity made a swift decision, her over-riding concern to keep Sammi as untraumatised as possible. Which meant sticking to her normal routine as much as she could. And which therefore meant that she was being steamrollered into including Benedict Jackson for breakfast.

Cursing the kindheartedness that had allowed him to sleep on her sofa instead of treating him with the kind of behaviour he merited and kicking him out of her flat, she gave him a chilly smile, making no effort to disguise her irritation.

'I'm going to shower now,' she told him, wishing that Sammi had not scampered off towards her bedroom and that she did not have to stare into attractive green eyes which were crinkling at the corners the way they used to a lifetime ago.

The precious secret that she had kept from him was forgotten; Jamie Brennan was forgotten. Everything was forgotten. All Benedict could think about right now was kissing her. He couldn't ever remember wanting to kiss a woman so much, not even Verity in those heady, early days of youthful passion. My, but her lips looked so soft and so sweet and—strangely innocent, too. And yet she had borne his child—*his* child! Something primitive and possessive stirred into life deep inside him.

'Are you?' he murmured huskily, his eyes telling her most definitely that he would like to share the shower with her.

Even *now*! Verity thought furiously. Even at a time like this all he could think about was sex! 'Yes!' she snapped, then drew her mouth into an affronted straight line and marched off in as prim and as outraged a manner as any hospital matron.

Except that no hospital matron had ever made Benedict ache the way he was aching right now. He went into the kitchen and filled the kettle, switching on the radio and trying to listen to the early-morning news when all he could wonder was how long Verity was going to *be* in the wretched shower for. Because if he didn't douse himself in cold water pretty soon his blood pressure was going to go shooting through the ceiling!

As breakfasts went it was disastrous. It was possibly the worst breakfast that Verity had ever presided over though, by a mutually unspoken agreement, nothing of any significance was discussed.

The toast got burned, the scrambled eggs were overcooked and then a strawberry yoghurt was knocked all over the kitchen floor and spattered everywhere.

'I didn't do it!' yelled Sammi.

'I didn't say you did!' answered Verity crossly. 'But you've just put the heel of your slipper in it!' She looked up to find Benedict watching the two of them closely, his eyes narrowed and masking his reaction to the slapstick that was taking place in the kitchen. Well, at least he now knows I'm not good wife material, she thought wryly, certainly not the kind of wife an ambitious man like Benedict would be looking for. But the self-deprecating thought hurt far more than she would have expected it to.

She reached for a cloth to wipe up the mess on the floor but Benedict forestalled her by grabbing the sponge from the draining-board.

'Here,' he said in that smooth, deep voice. 'Allow me.'

Verity shook her head. 'No, honestly. I couldn't—'

'You don't have to do it,' he cut in, and rinsed the cloth out beneath the tap with experienced hands. 'Just because you clean up after me in Theatre doesn't mean to say you have to do it when we're off duty.'

Verity bristled. There was no need to make her sound like some sort of servant! 'How very benevolent of you!'

The green eyes sparkled at her undisguised irritation. 'I thought so, too.'

Realising that she was overreacting to everything he said, Verity surveyed the pink, lumpy puddle that was spread all over the cheap linoleum floor and shuddered as she tried, and failed, to imagine the elegant Mr Jackson on his hands and knees clearing it all up. She gave him one last chance to rescind his offer. 'Are you *quite* sure you don't mind doing it?'

'*Quite* sure,' he mocked. To be frank he needed to do something to occupy his hands and his thoughts. He had a long list ahead of him this morning and normally he would be mentally focusing on the cases and their possible complications.

But this morning all that he could think about was Sammi—the child whose very existence he had been denied. And Verity—the woman who had deliberately kept the information from him. Dear heaven, he ought to *hate* her. But hate would not help his case—or Sammi's.

And as he stared at the denim shirt she wore tucked into closely fitting jeans he realised that he wanted to do something much more than hate her.

Denim was supposed to be thick and functional so why the hell was it emphasising those delicious curves as clearly as if she was still wearing her flimsy nightgown?

'It's such a mess,' she murmured, looking down, unsure of whether she meant the floor or the situation they found themselves in.

He smiled, deliberately obtuse. 'I know. Like blood—there's always more of the darned stuff when you spill it than ever there was in the syringe! Do you have any kitchen roll? And a bowl and something to clean it with?'

He was certainly a man used to giving orders but, try as she might, Verity was unable to be anything other than disarmed by his capability, just as she had been disarmed by the gifts he had brought last night before her dramatic revelation. She handed over everything he had asked for and watched him crouch down and begin to dispose of the yoghurt while she bemusedly made a pot of tea.

Sammi, meanwhile, was watching him intently, as an anthropologist might watch a newly discovered tribe.

'Blood, yuck!' Sammi observed conversationally. 'Do you see lots of blood in your job?'

'Oh, lots and lots and lots,' he answered benignly.

'Mummy never talks about the blood.'

'Neither do I, usually.'

'When were you my father?' Sammi drew her delicate, dark blonde eyebrows together and Verity gave a silent groan as she watched the five-year-old struggling to understand the complexities of grown-ups' behaviour.

Blast Benedict! she thought bitterly as she passed him a cup of tea. 'Just eat your breakfast up, Sammi,' she said quickly. 'We'll talk about it later. Now, we'd better get a move on or you'll be late for school.'

Benedict didn't know much about child-rearing but he had picked up enough from his sisters to know that children did not start school this early in the morning. He frowned. 'What time does she start school?'

'Not until nine. But I start work at seven-thirty. She goes to the childminder until then.' She saw his eyes narrow, saw Sammi take on a belligerent expression and was determined that *neither* of them should start objecting. 'So if you wouldn't mind hurrying, Sammi,' she said, 'otherwise we'll miss the bus.'

Benedict thought that he had misheard and frowned again. 'Bus?' he queried, as though Verity had just suggested hang-gliding into the hospital with Sammi attached to her by a delicate piece of string.

She knew what was coming and was determined to resist it. He had got his way over breakfast; he had better learn that she was not someone whom he could walk all over, no matter *what* the circumstances. 'Yes,' she answered coolly. 'Sammi and I always take the bus to work. She likes it and so do I—'

'But you always moan when it's late,' butted in

Sammi, her blue eyes even bigger with bewilderment.

'Cars cut you off and make you so isolated,' Verity rushed on. 'And it's so important to get fresh air, don't you think?'

'Absolutely,' he concurred smoothly. 'But not today, I don't think.'

'Why not?' she demanded stubbornly.

His green eyes glinted with devilment as he cocked his head in the direction of the window, where raindrops were trickling down the pane with depressing regularity. 'It's raining,' he pointed out gently.

'I love the——' But one look at both Sammi's and Benedict's faces made Verity decide not to pursue *that* particular line. Inspiration came. 'You drive a sports car!' she told him triumphantly.

'And how did you know that?' he queried.

Verity blushed; she actually *blushed*! 'One of the nurses happened to mention it——you know how excited some people get when a new doctor joins the staff!'

'But not you, Verity?' he probed.

She lifted her chin proudly. 'No. Not me.'

'My sports car has a small seat in the back and you're slim enough to fit in comfortably enough. Sammi can sit in the front and you can take her place when we've dropped her off.'

Verity decided to throw in the towel and accept his offer of a lift. 'Oh, very well,' she said ungratefully. 'But we need to leave in twenty minutes so, if you want to take a shower, you'd better get a move on.'

By the time he had stripped off for his shower all desire for her had fled and so Benedict stood beneath the streaming hot jets, throwing his dark head back, the water splashing luxuriously all over his muscle-packed, lightly tanned skin. He opened his lips and let the water rain noisily into his mouth and tried very hard not to think of Sammi growing up without knowing him or of Jamie Brennan and how deep his relationship with Verity went.

At times like this it was easier not to think of anything.

Verity snapped her seat belt into position and stared fixedly ahead while Benedict started up the engine, his knuckles white as he gripped the steering-wheel.

'Why on earth did you have to tell her?' she demanded as the powerful car ate up the miles.

His breath came thick and fast, his heart a painful hammering in his chest as he tried to control his temper. 'Why on earth didn't you tell *me*,' he retorted, 'that I had a daughter?'

'There was no reason to—*Benedict*!' she screamed as the car swerved to the left and he brought the car to a halt, only narrowly missing mounting the kerb. 'What do you think you're *doing*?'

'Avoiding an addition to the orthopaedic surgeon's morning list,' he snapped as he began winding the window down and beckoning to a terrified-looking teenager on a bicycle. 'Come here,' Benedict instructed quietly and, when the sheepish-looking youth had complied, subjected him to a lengthy reprimand that left the teenager thoroughly chastened. Verity knew with an unswerving certainty that he would never ride his bike without due care and attention on a busy highway again.

'And wear a blasted helmet in future!' was Benedict's parting comment.

'Y-yes, sir,' stammered the teenager, and rather obsessively checked both ways for traffic before he rode off.

When Benedict started the car up again a new tension crackled in the air.

Verity ran a distracted hand back through her thick blonde hair—unusually tousled and unruly this morning because she had had to dress in such a hurry *and* share her bathroom. There was so much to say that it was impossible to know where to start. And whatever she might feel inside, there was simply no good to be had from fighting with him. 'Benedict, listen—' she began tentatively.

'I'm listening to nothing!' he retorted savagely. 'I have a list to operate on and you've made me uptight enough already—'

'I've made *you* uptight?' she queried disbelievingly.

'That's what I said,' he growled. 'There's a sick neonate in Special Care after last night's Caesar; additional problems I can do without.'

'Like me scrubbing for you?' she challenged,

her heart contracting as she anticipated him saying that he could not work alongside her. Then she would be relegated to somewhere well out of his way, no doubt, put in with the general surgeon or the orthopod or, even worse, the day cases in minor ops.

He smoothly moved down into a lower gear. 'I wouldn't dream of changing that,' he answered coolly. 'You're excellent at your job and that's all I care about in Theatre.'

'And out of Theatre? What there?'

His mouth tightened. 'I presume you're referring to my daughter?'

Her heart contracted again, painfully this time, at the proprietorial way in which he referred to Sammi. 'You know I am,' she answered quietly.

'As I've already told you, I don't intend discussing the subject on a car ride into work,' he told her heatedly. 'That's the sort of thing that causes accidents.'

They were approaching the main road that led to the hospital and already Verity had seen a couple of people she knew. Luckily they had not seen her but someone was bound to in a minute. . . She cleared her throat. 'Benedict,' she whispered.

His hand tensed on the steering-wheel. When she spoke like that—so softly, with that husky little undertone making her voice sound wickedly sexy—he not only managed to put her deception out of mind but was also in danger of granting her anything she might ask of him. Great danger.

'What?' He deliberately made his voice as unforthcoming as possible.

'Can you stop the car here?'

He eased his foot off the accelerator immediately. 'Here? But we're miles away from the theatre block and it's still chucking it down.' His eyes narrowed as comprehension dawned. 'Oh, I see! You don't want anyone from the hospital seeing us together?'

Something in his tone made her inexplicably nervous. 'It just seemed the most sensible thing to do.'

'Did it?' he snarled, and renewed the car's considerable speed. 'And keeping Sammi a secret— tell me, did that seem the most sensible thing to do, too?'

It had; it honestly had—at the time. But one glance at Benedict's harsh and unforgiving profile told Verity that he was in no sort of mood for explanations. 'You implied that there wasn't enough time to discuss Sammi's future on the way to work,' she responded calmly. 'We'll talk about it some other time.'

The car screeched to a halt in the doctors' car park, and Benedict turned briefly to face her. 'When?'

'Tomorrow night?'

He shook his dark head firmly. 'Tonight.'

'Please?'

'Why should I,' he answered shortly, trying not to lose himself in those wide, aquamarine eyes, 'please *you*?'

Verity swallowed. 'What if I told you that I was tired; that you're tired; that Sammi's tired? That we're all emotionally strung out. That we have big decisions to make, quite apart from any recriminations which you might feel are in order. And that those kinds of decisions are best made, or discussed, after a good night's rest.'

He gave a brittle kind of laugh. 'And is that what you think we'll all get by postponing it? Eight hours of uninterrupted shut-eye?'

'Sammi might,' Verity answered evenly, 'even if we don't. And, besides, I need some time alone with her.'

He was perfectly still for a moment and then he nodded, leaning right across her to open the car door—his arm brushing against her knees as he did so. Verity was unable to stop the violent tremor that shivered down her spine at just that brief contact.

As his arm made contact with her knees Benedict watched her lips open slightly and then close into the cutest and most unintentional of pouts as the shudder of sensual awareness trembled through her. He knew enough about women to know that if he kissed her now she would make no resistance. But if he kissed her now he suspected that things might get out of control very quickly and he was much too old to start petting in public—especially in the doctors' car park.

And wouldn't making love to her complicate an already impossible situation? He gave the door a swift push before he could change his mind. 'Tomorrow it is, then,' he agreed curtly.

As she slid her long legs out of the car Verity was aware of the regret that washed over her in an unwelcome wave. Had she wanted him to kiss her? Yes, she had. She swallowed down her disappointment with difficulty. 'But I'll see you in Theatre, surely?'

'Yes,' he confirmed unwillingly.

Verity heard his reluctance and took off at speed while Benedict sat and watched her running into the hospital building just as he had done yesterday morning, a whole lifetime ago.

At that very moment the sun broke out—as if some celestial art director had willed it to—transforming the raindrops into a kaleidoscope of dazzling colour that arced magnificently against the grey sky.

But to Benedict the spectacle of the rainbow seemed insignificant when compared to the primrose blaze of Verity's hair.

'Oh, *blast* it!' he cursed loudly. 'Blast, blast and *blast* it!' And he pulled the keys violently out of the ignition.

CHAPTER SIX

'DID I see you getting out of Mr Jackson's car just now, Verity?' asked Julia Morris.

Verity pulled her bobbed hair back into a tight pony-tail and sighed. If only student nurse Morris applied as much energy and curiosity to the workings of the operating theatre as she did to the love lives of those who worked there then she had the makings of a future nurse manager!

But Verity wasn't the type of nurse who enjoyed pulling rank or causing a row so instead she merely gave a nod to her junior. 'Yes,' she said briefly, which to anyone with *any* degree of sensitivity would have indicated that she did not want to pursue the subject further.

Not so to Julia Morris. Julia was in the same set as Anna Buchan and two more different nurses you could not hope to find. Her brown eyes glinted with curiosity as she watched Verity push a stray strand of golden hair beneath her theatre cap. 'Does he live near you?'

Verity fell into the trap that she didn't even realise had been set. 'No,' she answered with a frown. 'He's living in the doctors' mess. I think.'

'Oh?' Julia's eyes bulged like a frog's with pure excitement. 'So he just *happened* to be passing your flat first thing, did he?' she queried slyly.

But by now Verity was past caring about what the hospital grapevine would make of all this. She had far more to worry about, she realised, than her reputation. 'That's right,' she lied but she superstitiously crossed her fingers as she said it.

'*Really?*' queried Julia insolently.

Refusing to get riled—for what good would that do her already shot nerves?—Verity gave a prim smile. '"*Really*",' she repeated mockingly.

'But won't Mr Brennan mind?' asked Julia slyly.

Verity met her gaze full on. 'And why should Mr Brennan mind?' she challenged.

It was clearly not the reaction that Julia had hoped for. So she tried another tack. 'He's *terribly* dishy, isn't he?'

She was persistent, she would say that for her! Verity retained her bland expression as she pushed her slim feet into her white clogs. 'Who? Mr Brennan?' she queried, deliberately misunderstanding.

Julia drew her thick brown brows together. 'Mr *Jackson*!' she corrected. 'And he's single!'

'Then I wish you all the luck in the world,' observed Verity evenly and was rewarded with an astonished expression on Julia's face, after which she lapsed into a kind of stunned silence then disappeared in the direction of the coffee-room.

Which left Verity wondering what to do next. Thanks to Benedict she had arrived much too early for work. Normally the staff all filed into the coffee-room for a drink and a chat before the list started.

Normally.

This wasn't normal and Verity didn't feel normal. It would be hell to have to sit and face Benedict as though there wasn't this great secret between them.

So she wouldn't. She would find out which list she was scrubbing for and then she would clean her theatre up. . .

'Verity!'

Verity turned to the shrill, familiar voice of Sister Saunders, who was beaming at her expansively.

'Glad to see that you took my little lecture to note,' the older woman smiled, and Verity blinked in confusion.

'Lecture?'

'About rushing into work at the last minute. You're bright and early this morning, aren't you, *and* with plenty of time to have a civilised start to the day before the list begins? Come and have some coffee—Gisela's assuming her usual matriarchal role and making some for everyone,' she chuckled.

'Sister, I don't really think—'

'Although,' and Sister Saunders lowered her voice as though Verity hadn't spoken, 'she's *especially* enthusiastic this morning. Yesterday Benedict brought in some of the most *wonderful* coffee I've ever tasted!'

Did he make a habit of that? wondered Verity.

Had he also provided the department with Belgian chocolates and macadamia nuts? And here she had been thinking that his gesture had been in some way special. 'I'd better not, Sister,' she said, but Sister Saunders was shaking her head in that decisive way of hers.

'Nonsense!' she boomed heartily. 'I shan't take no for an answer! If I were as slim as you I'd be eating all day! Which is probably why I'm not,' she added with a rueful note of insight as she patted her ample belly. 'Now, tell me, Verity,' she lowered her voice to a stage whisper as they approached the coffee-room. 'How do you rate him?'

Verity blinked. 'Who?'

'Mr Jackson!'

It took Verity a moment or two to realise that Sister Saunders meant professionally. 'Um—he seems very thorough,' she answered honestly. 'Fast yet neat. A textbook operator, I guess. Of course I haven't seen him tested yet so I can't judge how he would be in an emergency.' But she doubted that he would panic; people rarely got to senior registrar level unless they were able to cope in the most horrendous situations.

Sister Saunders looked at her with exasperation. 'That wasn't what I meant, my dear!'

'Wasn't it?' asked Verity innocently.

'I meant as a *man*!' rasped Sister.

Verity smiled at the older woman's indomitable matchmaking, slightly relieved that she *could* still smile and especially about a subject that was so sensitive. 'Oh, he's been given top marks for hunkiness by the juniors,' she answered airily.

'Julia Morris, I presume?' snorted Sister. 'That young woman would flutter her eyelashes at anyone with a Y chromosome in their body. *And* she talks too much!' She blinked her eyes innocently. 'Heard from Jamie, have you?'

Verity wondered what it might be like if your private life was actually *private*! 'Er—he rang up a couple of nights ago.'

'Having a good time, is he?'

'He says that Disneyland is everything they say it is and more and that Harriet loves it.' He had also said, at some length, that he missed her and that Sammi would have enjoyed Disneyland, too. Which Verity didn't doubt for a moment. It just made her feel a bit guilty about denying Sammi something that was most children's dream.

And of course then she hadn't encountered Benedict. . .

Sister Saunders pushed open the door to the coffee-room and Verity realised that there was no way in the world that she was going to be able to avoid seeing Benedict without exciting gossip in the department or bad feeling between the two of them. So she mentally girded herself to react calmly when she saw him, her eyes quickly sweeping around the room until she found him.

He was talking busily into the phone, one hand gesticulating as he barked out a series of questions, then nodded his head and put the phone down, his movements all athletic grace as he turned to face Verity.

Their eyes met for a long, silent moment and Verity realised that something fundamental between them had changed. The secret between them might be unspoken while they were at work but it was a secret shared. And whether or not Benedict blamed Verity for keeping Sammi's existence from him, nonetheless a bond existed now between her and the father of her child. And it—or rather, he—wasn't just going to go away, either, even if she wanted him to. And Verity wasn't at all sure that she wanted him to.

She poured coffee for herself and Sister and settled down on a chair by the window and tried very hard to nod her head and look interested when Barney Fisher, one of the anaesthetists, began telling her about a new vegetarian restaurant that had opened within walking distance of the hospital.

'We all ought to go there one night—a whole bunch of us,' Barney said, pushing his John Lennon spectacles back up his long, thin nose. 'Think it's a good idea, Sister?'

Sister Saunders smiled. 'You young ones go. I'm much too set in my ways. I'm sure that Gisela and Verity would be delighted to sample lentil stew or whatever it is they give you.'

Gisela nodded eagerly and Verity didn't bother saying anything since no one would probably get it together to organise it anyway!

'And how about you, Benedict?' grinned Barney. 'Game? Or are you strictly a meat and two veg man? I can somehow imagine you with a plateful of flesh that's almost crawling off the plate!'

'Meaning that he's macho and rugged-looking, I suppose?' defended Julia Morris gushingly, then blushed as she saw the brief but unmistakable look of irritation that Benedict flashed at her.

'I enjoy vegetarian food immensely,' Benedict told Barney with a smile. 'Count me in.'

'Ooh! Me, too!' chorused two of the recovery room nurses immediately and Verity rose soundlessly to her feet and went over to the sink with her coffee-cup. She was not about to witness the sight of every female in the hospital clamouring to be part of an outing just because it happened to include the delectable Mr Jackson!

But just as she tipped her half-drunk coffee down the sink there was the fast shrilling of a bleeper and Verity didn't have to hear the deep voice answering to guess that it was Benedict's. Nor to hear his rapid monosyllabic responses to know that it was serious.

He hurried out and Verity, having now jettisoned her cup of coffee for no reason whatsoever, gave him a couple of minutes to disappear and then left the room herself.

She went into Theatre looking for work and, after a determined hunt, managed to find two trolleys which had traces of dust around the wheels. These she wiped down thoroughly before checking all her packs of instruments off against the morning's list. It was boring but necessary work—and at least it kept her occupied.

Her heart sank slightly when Julia Morris came in, announcing gaily that, 'I'm your scrub nurse for the day! Lucky old you, Verity!'

Honestly! How could she be so nonchalant after virtually accusing Verity of spending the night with the new senior registrar? The girl had the skin of a rhinoceros, Verity decided as she held a small silver-coloured kidney dish out to be filled up with normal saline.

Barney popped his head round the door of the anaesthetic room which led directly into Theatre. 'The first patient is on his way up,' he said. 'Where's our surgeon?'

'Here,' came an instantly recognisable voice from across the theatre and then Benedict walked in and Verity was shocked by his outward appearance.

She knew immediately that he must have had bad news, less from the lack of colour in his face than by the hard, heavy set of his shoulders. She watched the muscles beneath the thin blue material of his top bunching together in tension and she felt an undeniable urge to go to him; to take him into her arms; to rub all that tension away beneath her fingertips.

Verity suddenly forgot all her good intentions about keeping work and private lives separate. She moved blindly away from her trolley and walked over to him, not even aware of Julia Morris's huge, wide eyes watching them.

'What's happened?' she asked softly.

He rubbed at his temples distractedly. 'That emergency I had in the middle of the night, remember?'

Verity nodded, now only *too* aware of Julia's excited inrush of breath as she mused on the implications behind *that* remark.

'The mother was doing just fine, given the circumstances,' he told her heavily. 'Until about half an hour ago when she started complaining of calf pain. She was on a heparin drip—everything. And then she died in front of us.' His voice shook very slightly. 'There was nothing we could do—'

'What happened?' asked Verity, shocked.

'A massive embolism, most probably—maybe from one of the pelvic veins, although we'll need the post-mortem to confirm. Her husband was waiting outside. He'd just come back from Special Care. At least the baby's still alive. . .just.' The green eyes were bleak as they stared at Verity without seeing her. 'There was nothing we could do to help her,' he finished bitterly. 'Nothing.'

Julia's eyes were huge. 'Gosh, Mr Jackson,' she asked unwisely. 'Do you *always* get so involved with your patients?'

From the filthy look he gave her Verity knew that she had better intervene before she had a bust-up on her hands. 'Just let Mr Jackson get scrubbed in peace, would you, Nurse Morris? Perhaps you could make yourself useful and go into the anaesthetic room and find out if the patient has been intubated yet?' she asked with crisp authority.

When Julia had gone she gave him a long, rueful look. 'Anything I can get you?'

His eyes refocused on her oval face, so serene and undemanding. He had forgotten just what easy company she could be. 'Anything at all?' he queried.

She smiled. 'Within reason.'

'That nurse was right, you know; I don't normally react this way when one of my patients dies—however shocking or unexpected.' He frowned and narrowed his eyes, the ebony sweep of his lashes completely obscuring the brilliant colour. 'I don't want to have to wait until tomorrow for an explanation, Verity,' he told her baldly. 'I want to get it sorted out as soon as possible. Tonight, whether it's prudent or not. I don't care.'

And she could understand that. She, too, had been rather regretting her earlier decision to wait. How much peace of mind would either of them get if they waited? She nodded. 'OK, Benedict. Tonight it is. But let me put Sammi to bed first.'

Before he could reply the door from the anaesthetic room swung inwards and Julia reappeared, her brown eyes quickly darting from one to the other. Almost as though she expected to find the two of us kissing, thought Verity with acid amusement.

'The patient has just gone under,' she announced, using the slang term for anaesthesia.

Benedict put the taps on full blast and doused his arms and elbows in water before squirting a huge dollop of pink antiseptic soap into the palm

of his hand. 'Thanks,' he said briefly, so quietly
that only Verity could hear, and she wondered
whether it was her imagination or did his voice
sound unbearably bleak?

The patient was lying on the table by the time
he approached, his gloved hands raised in the air
as if in supplication and his gown flapping open.

Julia sprang to the rescue. 'Shall I tie your gown
for you, Mr Jackson?'

He glanced around the theatre in mock question.
'Unless the good fairy's going to float down from
out of nowhere and do it then I suggest you'd
better,' he said sarcastically, and Julia flushed.

Verity glanced up from her where she was laying all her instruments in neat lines on the sterile
cloth which covered her trolley. Julia might be
intensely irritating, yes, and Benedict might be
upset but there was really no excuse for him to
talk to the juniors like that.

He sensed her watching him and looked up.
Green eyes clashed with an accusing aquamarine
blaze and he gave a small shrug as he took her
silent reprimand in.

That was the last thing he needed—Verity acting as his conscience—but, having said that, as
reproaches went it was fairly irresistible! He turned
to the student nurse beside him who immediately
sucked her cheek-bones and her stomach in and
he hid a smile. He didn't want her passing out on
them through lack of oxygen to the blood!

'Forgive me for biting your head off, Nurse. . .?'
he queried.

'Morris!' gushed Julia, pleased that she had skipped breakfast that morning. She might not be as slim as Verity Summers, she thought triumphantly, but she was a good five years younger *and* she didn't have a child at home with no husband!

'Morris,' Benedict echoed blandly. 'Lack of sleep always makes me grouchy.'

'That's OK,' answered Julia. 'Busy night was it?'

A sardonic green glance shimmered across the table. 'You could say that,' he answered.

Verity felt her cheeks growing pink. Why wouldn't he stop looking at her like that? And fancy giving Julia all the ammunition she needed to have the news around the hospital by lunchtime that the new surgeon had spent the night at *her* flat! She could have wept—because this really *was* a case of all smoke without fire. Benedict hadn't laid one finger on her!

Benedict performed two D and Cs—Dilatation and Curettage—of the uterus. The first was done for a young woman of twenty-four who had miscarried at sixteen weeks and was done routinely in such cases where products of the lost pregnancy might have been retained in the woman's womb.

'This is her third miscarriage,' said Benedict, frowning. 'She's desperate for a baby, too. Looks like a Shirodkar suture next time round.'

'What's a Shirodkar suture?' asked Julia Morris eagerly.

Benedict thought that if the girl stood much closer to him they would be joined at the hip.

While the only woman he *wanted* to be joined at the hip with was standing as cool and as aloof as if he had not been in the room. He shifted his weight away from the student nurse. 'Ask Verity,' he suggested mildly. 'I'm sure she'll be able to tell you all about Shirodkar sutures.'

Verity took a used swab from him, thinking that he could be the devil himself. She somehow doubted whether Julia was at all interested in learning; she certainly hadn't shown any great tendency to ask questions before the arrival of Mr Jackson! But it *was* obvious that she wanted Benedict to tell her and not Verity. Still.

'It's a treatment for cervical incompetence,' she said. 'Which this woman clearly has. Cervical incompetence is when a woman is unable to carry a baby to term, usually for reasons unknown. So the doctor puts in an unabsorbable suture, which is placed around the internal os of the cervix. This is usually done during the early stages of pregnancy. The patient is then allowed to go to full term and normal labour follows when the stitch is removed. Is that clear?' Verity raised her eyebrows questioningly and Julia gave a brief nod, rushing forward to untie Benedict's gown.

The next case up was Ethel, their very own sandwich lady, who was having a hysteroscope— where a telescope-like instrument was passed through the vagina and into the uterus. This investigation was generally performed under general anaesthetic and in Ethel's case it was to discover the causes of her irregular bleeding with periods which had been coming at two to three week intervals.

Verity's gaze idly drifted towards the door as Barney and his nurse wheeled the unconscious patient through from the anaesthetic room. 'How's Ethel?' she asked him.

'Sleeping like a baby,' smiled Barney. 'Lovely lady, Ethel! Always gives me any leftover sandwiches at the end of the day!'

'So *she's* the one who's responsible for our spreading hips!' giggled the anaesthetic nurse.

Benedict's eyes glinted as they lingered on the lower part of Verity's body. Oh, really? he mocked silently, but then he remembered the laughter lines around Ethel's careworn face when she had informed him last evening that he had eaten her favourite staff nurse's sandwich and flirtation was forgotten.

He hadn't seen her in Clinic himself; Jamie had. But he knew what diagnosis the consultant suspected. Please don't be what I suspect it to be, he thought as he watched Julia slide the patient's legs into the position known as the lithotomy position which gave the surgeon easiest access to the vagina.

Very carefully Benedict inserted the hysteroscope through the vagina and into the uterus and, after visually examining the area, he passed a slim instrument down the hysteroscope which enabled him to snip off some tissue samples.

'Let's get this biopsy off to Histology, can we?'

he asked crisply when the samples were safely
deposited in labelled, sterile pots.

Next up he had two repair operations for prolapse of the uterus, one of which turned out to be
a lot more complicated than he had anticipated,
and by the time lunchtime arrived Benedict was
exhausted.

He was reluctant to go and eat his sandwich in
the coffee-room; he wanted to be alone with his
thoughts.

He put a spare white coat on over his theatre
suit and took the lift all the way down to the main
entrance of the hospital, buying a can of cold cola
and a sandwich from the shop in the foyer and
taking it out into the garden.

The architect of St Jude's had been a man with
an extravagant imagination, which a generous
benefactor had allowed him to freely indulge. The
hospital was built on the lines of an old-fashioned
castle with four large wings forming a central
square, in the midst of which was the courtyard of
paths, flower-beds and small lawns that formed
the famous hospital garden.

Considering that it was in the middle of London
the garden was an oasis of calm and peace. Mature
shrubs and trees had been planted during the hospital's two-hundred year history and it boasted
one of the finest mulberry trees in all England.
Volunteers regularly gave their time to tend to
the perfectly manicured lawns and it was part of
St Jude's policy that patients on rehabilitation
should be given what was known as 'practical

physiotherapy'—gentle tasks, such as dead-heading flowers, which helped their progress and helped the hospital, too!

Today the last of the daffodils were waving their serated yellow trumpets in the light, warm breeze. The sun blazed down and above Benedict's dark head the sky was the brightest, clearest blue that he could ever remember seeing. He recalled a line from a poem he'd learnt as a boy, 'all in the blue unclouded weather'. And then wondered what on earth had prompted him to bring to mind Tennyson's romantic yet ultimately tragic story of the Lady of Shalott.

But maybe that was what the discovery of progeny did to you. Made you aware of your own mortality so that your senses became finely tuned. He couldn't remember ever having lived in the moment the way he was doing just now.

He stared at his sandwich without enthusiasm.

Just how much of Sammi, he wondered, was Verity prepared to let him have?

CHAPTER SEVEN

SAMMI was settled in bed and Verity had just finished changing when she heard Benedict at the door.

She gave the sitting room one final, satisfied glance before going to the front door. One thing was for sure. He certainly would not be able to make any snide comments about the state of the place tonight, she thought. Every toy was packed neatly away and not a mug or a book littered any of the gleaming surfaces.

She had even managed to stop off at the market after she had collected Sammi from the child-minder's and had bought a huge armful of flowers at a fraction of their normal price. Already they were in full bloom and in a day or two the flowers would be dead but, for tonight at least, they transformed the flat into a scented heaven. Daisies and roses, freesias and lilies—she had arranged them artistically in vases made out of the blue-coloured glass she collected and had dotted them all round the sitting room. It might not be large or luxurious, Verity thought defiantly, but at least it's home.

She pulled the door open and there stood Benedict, slightly grim-faced. No gifts tonight, she thought. 'Hi.'

'Hello.'

'You'd better come in.'

'Thanks.'

He glanced from right to left, ridiculously disappointed not to see the butter-haired angel. 'Is Sammi in bed?'

Verity fiddled with the tiny silver ring on her little finger, the oddest pang shooting through her as she observed his reaction. 'Of course. She's always in bed by seven. Well,' she amended, with a slight smile. '*Nearly* always! Can I get you some coffee?'

'Do you have any beer?'

'I think so.'

'A beer would be great.'

While she was clattering around in the kitchen fetching the beer Benedict sat down in one of the chairs and looked around. It amused and rather touched him to see that she had obviously gone to a lot of trouble tidying the flat up—it was barely recognisable as the same place he had walked into last night. And the flowers were glorious.

Verity handed him a bottle of beer and a glass—which he declined—but was unprepared for his next question.

'Who bought you the flowers?'

'I bought them myself.'

He took a long mouthful of beer, drinking it directly from the bottle like a cowboy in a film, his eyes never leaving her face as his tongue flicked out to remove the slick of white froth that outlined his upper lip. 'A woman shouldn't have to buy her own flowers,' he observed deliberately.

Which Verity thought was beside the point. He was even *sounding* like a cowboy now! And the last thing she wanted was to go all weak at the knees at such brazen masculinity. She didn't reply but sat in the opposite chair sipping at her fruit juice, her ankles locked primly together.

'Doesn't *Jamie* buy you flowers?'

'That isn't any of your business.'

'Isn't it?'

'No.'

Benedict was discovering another new emotion. Jealousy. He felt some thunderous black cloud invade his mind and it was not a sensation he enjoyed one little bit.

There was an angry silence for a long moment until Benedict finally sat back and looked at her squarely, his face suddenly serious—flowers and Jamie forgotten. Only one thing was important, he reminded himself. One thing. 'Will you tell me about it?' he asked.

'How much do you want to know?'

Not want, he thought, suddenly urgent—*need* to know. 'Everything,' he said quietly. 'Tell me everything.'

They were, she realised suddenly, talking in the kind of shorthand normally used by a couple who had been together for years. And things like that could stir foolish hope in the heart of a woman who should know better.

'It's almost impossible to know where to begin. . .' She looked at him hopefully but he did not say a word. It was initially difficult to talk openly about something which she had kept concealed for so long and particularly difficult when it had to be done while facing the other protagonist and that steady, green stare of his.

'After we——' she faltered, then tried again. 'After you left St Thomas's I carried on pretty much as normal.' Well, her behaviour would have been stretching most people's conception of normality, but still. . .

There was no need to tell him of the bucket of tears that she had cried over him late into the night, every night. Or the fact that she had been so distraught that she had put the lateness of her period down to the stress of Benedict leaving. But when her breasts had grown swollen and acutely tender she had been unable to hide the truth from herself any longer. 'And then I discovered that I was pregnant,' she said quietly.

'That must have been pretty traumatic.' Benedict spoke almost to himself, holding onto the bottle of beer as if it was a lifeline.

'Something of an understatement,' she observed rather drily. 'But, yes, I suppose you could say that it was traumatic.'

He put the beer bottle down as he heard her speak in that wooden little voice, his face suddenly alive and vibrant and accusing and angry. 'But why the hell didn't you contact me, Verity? *Tell* me!' he demanded hotly.

Verity chose her words carefully. 'What would have been the point? We had split up. There was no love between us——'

His mouth hardened. 'The point,' he emphasised slowly, 'was that as the father I bore a certain responsibility towards you——'

Verity's chin went up sharply in defiance and the moon-pale hair sparked silken fire at the sudden movement. 'But I didn't want to be your *responsibility*!' she retorted proudly, but he shook his head in a remonstrative way that made her feel, most peculiarly, ashamed. 'That's why!'

'You shouldn't have shut me out like that,' he objected quietly. Shouting wasn't going to solve anything. 'I should have shared it with you. Didn't it ever occur to you that I had a *right* to know?'

The secret, the second secret that she had locked away inside her for six long years, began to clamour loudly to be heard until she could no longer ignore it. 'But I tried,' she stumbled hoarsely, 'to contact you.'

He froze at something hidden in her voice. 'You did?' he queried suspiciously.

She remembered why she had deliberately stowed the memory away. Because it hurt. It hurt like hell. Even now. 'I travelled all the way to Manchester to talk to you,' she gulped. 'I was going to have you paged but one of the other doctors said that he thought you were in. I thought that it might be a good idea to see your instinctive reaction to the news that I was pregnant—without you being warned that I was there. He directed me to your room. So I went up. . .'

She looked up and into his face and Benedict felt some awful foreboding ice his skin as he read the truth in her eyes. Oh, my God. . . 'Verity, don't! Please, don't—'

'I went up,' she continued with dogged determination, as though each word wasn't cutting into her heart like a machete, 'and knocked. But there was no answer. So I naturally assumed there was no one in,' she added brightly. 'Anyway, I knocked once more and I heard someone call something, and I walked right in. . .'

He was caught in the blaze of reproach that sparked from her aquamarine eyes and he discovered that what he felt was genuine dismay. And shame. He shook his head to halt her. 'Verity, please—don't—'

'I walked in,' she cut across his words ruthlessly, triumphant to see his discomfiture as he anticipated what she was going to say next, 'only I quickly realised that you were in bed.' She swallowed down the bile which had come up with the memory. 'And not alone.'

'Dear God,' he whispered in horrified shock as he struggled to come to terms with how she must have felt. He hadn't even seen her. 'Verity, I'm so very—'

'No!' Her voice rang out. 'Please don't apologise to me, Benedict. There really isn't any need. Our relationship had finished some months before, after all, so why *shouldn't* you have had a new girlfriend?'

He gave a weary sigh. He remembered the other woman well—a junior doctor who had seemed to have everything that he thought he wanted in a woman. Except that she did not have Verity's unique ability to make him laugh. In her arms he had not found the peace that Verity had given him, only he had been too damned young and stubborn to accept that at the time. He sighed. 'And that was it? The only time you tried to get in touch?'

She fixed him with a withering look. 'What the hell did you expect, Benedict? That I'd mount a patrol outside your door until the coast was clear? No. It was clear that *I* had no room in your life any more and you certainly didn't look as though you were ready to cope with rattles and nappies and a child who was waking up every two hours during the night!'

'Point taken,' he accepted quietly, and was silent for a moment before he continued. 'So what did you do?'

She gave a tight, forced smile. 'I went to see my doctor, who strongly recommended a course of action which I found totally unacceptable.'

Their eyes met. He felt curiously and profoundly shocked. 'You mean. . .?'

'Yes,' she replied, remembering the revulsion that she had felt when the doctor had suggested that she might want to terminate her pregnancy. 'It never occurred to me. Not for a moment.'

'Thank you,' he said simply.

Which filled her heart with a sort of glow which she did her utmost to quell. 'I found another doctor, close to St Thomas's, and she referred me to a type of agency—'

'What kind of agency?'

Verity smiled. 'Oh, society has turned full circle, it seems. Girls who get pregnant outside marriage are no longer scorned and ostracised; they're positively encouraged to have their babies and given any help they might need in order to do so. That's the theory, anyway!

'I was given a place to stay. In Cornwall.' She closed her eyes on a dreamy memory. Pregnancy protected and cocooned you from reality and despite her obvious predicament of having no husband or money it had been a wonderful time in her life. 'It was very beautiful, actually. And quiet. Apart from the sound of the sea. I just used to sit there, on the rocks, for hours and hours, listening to the waves as they lapped over the sand. Feeling my baby kick inside me.'

The memory became as real as the present day. She found that her hands had automatically crept to cover her belly in that instinctively protective way that pregnant women have.

With a start she opened her eyes and was taken aback by the deep remorse she saw glittering in the depths of his eyes. Whatever else she had meant to do by talking to Benedict it had certainly not been to rake up a catalogue of his supposed crimes and then beat him up with them. 'It was a long time ago, Benedict,' she whispered softly.

Benedict swallowed, still reeling from how bitter he felt at his exclusion from Sammi's life. The way that Verity had said 'my baby' in that slumberous, possessive way had really brought it home to him. With an effort he kept his voice steady. 'So you've done it all—on your own?'

'Yes.'

'And what about your parents? Didn't they help you?'

Verity forced a smile. It sounded so ridiculously melodramatic to say it, like something from the last century. 'My parents disowned me when I told them that I was having a baby and that marriage wasn't an option. Hence the agency.'

Shock waves shuddered through him. 'And then what?' he shot out, biting down the urge to swear long and loud at the smallmindedness of her parents. He had only met them once, with their small, pinched faces and their disapproving looks, so unlike their vibrant, beautiful daughter.

Verity pushed a wayward strand of blonde hair back behind her ear. 'I stayed in Cornwall until Sammi was nearly a year old,' she told him. 'So we had that uninterrupted bonding time together. I helped run the crèche at the centre but it was only a temporary measure—they weren't really in a position to offer me the post permanantly. And, besides, I decided that I couldn't afford to let my nursing skills lapse or I would have no security for our future. I loved the country but London was where the work was.

'And so I came back. That's why I chose Theatre—it was one of the few stimulating options that gave me the opportunity to work regular hours.

'And here,' she finished flippantly because flippancy seemed to be something that she could safely hide behind, 'I am.'

'But you didn't come back to St Thomas's?'

'No,' she answered quietly.

'You chose a hospital where nobody knew you,' he guessed accurately.

'That's right.' Verity picked up her juice and sipped at it before replacing it on the table. 'I didn't want people judging me or feeling sorry for me or basically involving themselves in my life.'

'Apart from Jamie Brennan, of course?'

She met the unjust accusation in his eyes with equanimity. 'That's right,' she agreed softly, not caring when she saw the look of fury which crossed his face. Let him think what he liked. And let him feel angry, too! How many women had *he* had over the years? And yet she was supposed to have joined a nunnery, was she?

The jealousy coiled in the pit of his stomach like a small, black snake and Benedict mentally willed it away. Instead he thought how beautiful she looked as he watched her fold her arms over her small, high breasts in an unconscious gesture of self-protection. She was wearing a deceptively simple white shirt and an amazing short, pleated, black skirt which came midway down her thigh. She didn't look in the least bit mumsy.

With her face almost completely free of make-up and her hair swinging shiny and clean around her chin, she looked so young, so. . .pure, he decided almost reluctantly, that it was hard to believe that she had given birth to a child—*his* child—alone and in the most difficult of circumstances.

'And does anyone at St Jude's know?'

She raised her eyebrows questioningly, unwilling to help him out. 'Know what exactly, Benedict?'

He saw the challenge that sparked in her aquamarine eyes and he found it an unbearable turn-on but he repressed it immediately. There were far more important things than sex on his mind right now. 'About Sammi,' he said baldly.

'Well, I haven't kept my child hidden away all these years,' said Verity.

There it was again, he thought, *my* child. Didn't she know, or care, how much that hurt?

'If you mean do they know about her father. . .' Verity blushed as she said the word and looked down, unable to meet his eyes. There was something terribly intimate about calling him Sammi's father. 'Then, no,' she concluded baldly. 'They don't.'

He closed his eyes and rubbed at his temples, the way he always did when he was deep in thought, and when he opened them again he leaned forward as if physically attempting to bridge the huge chasm of misunderstanding that lay between them. 'Why did you tell me, Verity? Why now— after all these years?'

She chose her words carefully—she had had enough time during her sleepless night while Benedict slept on her sofa to consider what her answer to this particular question should be. 'Because I saw you,' she said simply, and bit her lip.

He waited; he could sense that she was on the brink of tears. His instinct was to pull her into his arms but he knew that he needed to tread very carefully—they were both on an emotional see-saw as it was. Eventually he prompted, 'And when you saw me? What?'

'You looked so like her. Well, not really *like* her. It's just—this way you have of raising your eyebrows. Both of you. That's what brought it home to me. Eyebrows! It sounds so silly now but I knew that morally I simply *had* to tell you. It sounds so silly,' she repeated helplessly and burst into tears.

He moved to the sofa in seconds, pulling her into his arms, and her head went straight away to his shoulder as though only his shoulder could relieve her of the most unbearable burden as she cried her heart out.

And Benedict felt as though he had been broken in two as his arms tightened to cradle her even closer against him. He had always been the kind of man to be unaffected, even irritated, by a woman's tears which over the years he had had turned on him in pique or in temper but mainly in frustration because he had not loved the women in his life as they had professed to love him.

But these tears. . . Dear Lord in heaven, he thought desperately, impossibly touched by her grief. These were so different.

'Not silly,' he murmured against the scented sweetness of her hair. 'Oh, no. Not silly at all, my—' He had been about to say 'darling' but he stopped himself in time. It would have been inappropriate, given the circumstances, and Verity would have been perfectly justified in slapping him very hard around the face if he'd started murmuring sweet nothings into her ears.

In her sorrow she heard nothing; instead she just cried until there were no tears left—tears which she hadn't allowed herself the indulgence of crying since she was newly pregnant. And by the time that they had become shuddering sobs Benedict seemed to have settled her back down on the sofa, a clutch of tissues pressed into her hand, and suddenly he was not there any more.

She heard him clanking around in the kitchen and when he returned it was with a tray of tea and he was smiling. And goodness only knew what he had to *smile* about!

'What's so funny?' she demanded.

He put the tray down and held one of Sammi's drawings aloft. It was a child's painting of yellow tulips in a blue glass jar, crude but highly imaginative. It had been stuck to the front of the fridge with three teddy-bear magnets. 'It's wonderful!' he exclaimed enthusiastically. 'Absolutely wonderful!'

Verity smiled softly at the undisguised pleasure in his voice. 'I think she's good, too,' she agreed. 'Of course, I know I could be biased.'

'You and me both,' said Benedict indulgently. 'My father was a brilliant amateur artist—he's a little too arthritic to paint in any degree of comfort now. But I wonder whether she takes after him?'

They stared at each other in silence.

'Sammi's never met any of her grandparents,' said Verity, on what sounded suspiciously like the beginnings of another sob.

Benedict handed her a cup of steaming, strong tea—more to distract her than anything else. His shirt was still wet from the last bout of crying! 'That can all be resolved,' he told her gently. 'At least on her paternal side. If that's what you want—but I'm rather assuming that it is.'

Verity drank her tea silently, not sure about what it was that she wanted, and when she looked up he read the confusion in her eyes as she tried to imagine his parents' response to learning that they were grandparents.

'You explained why you told me that I was Sammi's father but you didn't explain where you expected that admission to lead,' said Benedict slowly. 'You weren't just expecting to tell me and then for me to quietly go away, were you, Verity?' he quizzed softly, as he came to sit beside her.

'I don't know,' she admitted honestly. 'I didn't really think it through at all.' Her voice trembled as she found the courage to voice her thoughts. 'What do *you* want, Benedict?'

He paused, momentarily taken aback by the generous way she had asked him. He considered his reply. 'I want,' he said carefully, 'to get to know Sammi and for her to get to know me. And I would like to introduce her to my parents—'

'But not yet?' pleaded Verity.

He shook his head. 'When depends entirely on

when you think she's ready. Or able. And when *you're* ready. That might not be for months but I'm prepared to wait for as long as it takes.' He ran his hand back through the rich, dark hair—a gesture which Verity recognised of old.

His expression was very intense as he looked at her. 'You see, the thing is, Verity, that having introduced me to Sammi, giving me the first taster of being her father, has got me absolutely hooked.'

Verity gave him a quizzical look. 'Just like that?'

He nodded. 'Just like that. And if you're expecting me to just go away again, to quietly fade into the background, then I'm afraid you're going to be disappointed.'

She had to ask him. She *must*. 'And, apart from your parents, is there. . .anyone else who will be getting involved with my daughter?'

His black brows almost met in the middle of his forehead as he stared at her with bemusement. 'I'm not sure I follow you.'

She managed to convince herself that she was asking for Sammi's sake, and hers alone but still the question stuck in her throat like a fishbone. 'Is—? Are you involved with anyone?' she croaked. 'Married, perhaps?' She saw him frown again. 'A wife?' she queried, aware that she was overstressing her case but she didn't care. She wanted him to spell it out. If there was some woman—a fiancée or even a wife tucked away in the background—then she wanted to hear it. Now.

'''A *wife*''?' he repeated. Her words seemed to

anger him because the green eyes became flinty and his mouth tight. 'No, there isn't!' he snapped, and Verity was taken aback by the huge surge of relief that his words provoked. He eyed her with something approaching dislike.

'Is that how little you think of me?' he demanded. 'I asked you out for dinner before I knew anything about Sammi. Do you think that's how I would treat my wife? By making passes at attractive nurses on my first day at a new hospital?' He saw something written in her eyes then and gave a hollow, knowing laugh.

'Oh, I see,' and he nodded his head understandingly. 'You're basing your assumption on my past behaviour, are you, Verity?'

She realised that perhaps she was not being fair to him. He *might* have changed.

And as she had tried to convince herself over and over again, the two of them *had* broken up ages before she found him in the arms of another woman. She found her eyes drawn to the hard, flat lines of his cheek-bones, to the strong curve of his jaw which was so like Sammi's, and she did something that she had not done for years.

She flirted with him.

'Is that what you were doing?' she asked him softly. 'Making a pass at me?'

His mouth lost something of its hardness; this was a game he was a past master at. But anger still sharpened the edges of his attraction towards her. He leant forward. 'I should be careful, if I were you, Verity,' he warned softly. 'If you issue sensual, unspoken invitations like that then I'll take you up on them.'

'Benedict. . .' she whispered, on a half-hearted protest.

It would have been the easiest thing in the world to take her in his arms right then and kiss her. He knew very well how much she wanted him to. And he would. But not yet. This was much too precarious to be rushed by passion. For the first time ever he started re-inventing the rules by which he had lived his life. His reply was a teasing murmur. 'What?'

Verity swallowed—cursing him, hating him, wanting him. She felt raw, exposed, as if she had lain her heart bare for him to see. And she ached, too. She had repressed her sexuality and her desires for almost six arid years. And here was the man who had awakened both, the only man she had ever lain with. And they had a child together. Would it be so wrong? So very wrong? 'You *know*,' she told him angrily and made to stand up but he stopped her with a decisive shake of the dark head.

'Oh, yes, I know,' he whispered. 'You want me to kiss you.'

Her frustration was so strong that she said the unthinkable. 'Then why don't you? I'm not stopping you,' she said, unaware that her voice held a husky note of invitation which he found irresistible, and Benedict moved forward, took her face between his hands and stared down at her for a long, long moment, lost in the aquamarine glory of her eyes.

And Verity discovered that feelings for him, which she had thought she had eliminated, had simply lain dormant for all these years. Was she in danger of getting badly hurt for a second time?

She made to move away but this time Benedict pulled her insistently into his arms, reluctant to pass up on an opportunity to do what he had wanted to do since he'd first set eyes on her yesterday.

He lowered his head and kissed her, unhurriedly and experimentally, his mouth brushing lingeringly over the fullness of her lips.

It was so slow and yet so complete. Verity felt the world tip on its axis as he continued with his sensual exploration. With a little cry she opened her mouth beneath his, allowing his tongue to sweetly penetrate, to dart in and out and to lick at her until she felt quite dizzy with sensation. Her hands went up to grip at his broad shoulders and she felt her breasts grow heavy as she allowed herself to sink back against the cushions.

And Benedict came with her, his weight heavy and hard as his body engulfed hers, still kissing her all the while.

He felt the jut of her burgeoning breasts and stifled a moan of temptation. Oh, but he wanted her. So badly. He wanted all things. To tear the restrictive clothes from her body and take her in an instant. And yet to spend all the time in the world—to undress her degree by teasing degree, to love her so slowly. . .

He felt the jerky little push of her hips against him as her body instinctively responded to the

growing need in him and the reality of what he
was about to do appalled him. To take her now,
after everything that had happened. When she was
at her most tender, her most vulnerable. What kind
of man was he?

And if they made love now; started a relationship which might well fizzle into nothing—what
would come out of that for Sammi other than complications and confusion?

For all their sakes he should desist.

With the greatest effort of will he could remember making in his life he stopped kissing her and
stood up abruptly, going over to the mantelpiece
on the pretext of examining a photograph of
Sammi but in reality staring sightlessly at the
butter-coloured curls and the hyacinth-blue eyes.
Instead he concentrated on slowing down his loud,
ragged breathing. He thought of cold showers and
baths of ice-cubes—a device that he hadn't had to
employ since his schooldays.

And only when he was certain that he could
trust himself to turn around and face her without
being enticed into carrying her off to the nearest
bed did he do so.

Verity watched him turn, her eyes searching his
face for some clue of what might have motivated
that passionate kiss but all her hopes—if hopes
they were—faded and died the moment she saw
his features set into unforgiving lines, the eyes as
impassive as a statue's. And she shivered.

Benedict did not refer to it. He needed to get
out of there. And fast. Before he changed his mind.

'It's time I was going,' he said evenly and then he added, 'Do you have a photograph I could have? Of Sammi?'

'Of course I have!' Feeling ridiculously pleased, she went over to the drawer and fished around in it until she had found Sammi's recent school photo.

'Thanks.' He took it and smiled, then put it in his wallet. 'Now. About Sammi?' He raised his dark brows questioningly—that selfsame expression which had first so reminded her of their daughter.

'"About Sammi",' she repeated woodenly, like a child learning her times-tables.

'How about this coming weekend? I'm not on call. Are you free?'

Verity swallowed. Yes, she was free. She nodded, still not trusting herself to speak any sense.

'Then how about Saturday? I could come round early—we could make a day of it. That's if Sammi doesn't object,' he added.

Verity couldn't fault him. As a 'new' father he was making all the right noises. If only she felt as impartially about him as he seemed to about her then everything would be just fine and dandy. She nodded her affirmation once more.

Benedict frowned, marginally irritated by the aquamarine eyes looking almost wounded and disproportionately huge in a face suddenly drained of colour. Why the hell was she staring at him as though he were some big, bad ogre? He gave a heavy sigh and then adopted what he hoped was a conciliatory approach. 'Listen, Verity,' he said.

'It was a mistake just now. Heat of the moment, lust, hormones—whatever you want to call it—'

'Sex,' she put in baldly, pleased to see him wince very slightly. 'That's all it is.' That's all it ever was, she wanted to add but she would never do that. To say that would somehow be to devalue Sammi's existence. And it had never been just sex for her, oh, no. Verity had loved Benedict very much and she suspected that that love was only a flicker away from re-ignition.

So she had better dampen it. For her sake and, more importantly, for Sammi's.

Benedict started for the door, his mouth tasting as stale as if he had been eating cold cinders and all Verity's sweetness suddenly gone away. He turned around, his eyes veiled. 'Until Saturday, then,' he said.

But Verity shook her head. 'Until tomorrow, you mean. We still have to work together, remember?'

He gave a brief nod at the reminder. Yet another reason to stay away from her emotionally.

CHAPTER EIGHT

'FORCEPS! *Forceps, please*, Staff Nurse,' growled Benedict and Verity realised, to her absolute horror, that she had been miles away.

'S-sorry,' she stumbled and quickly slapped the instrument into his gloved hand.

There was a tense, awkward silence and then Benedict said, in tones of frozen ice, 'I asked you for a pair of forceps, Verity. This happens to be a retractor!'

'Oh, heck!' said Verity, half beneath her breath, and gave him the forceps instead although, from the grim-looking expression that still tightened his mouth, anyone would think that she had just handed him a time bomb!

From above his mask a pair of green eyes bored into her. 'If I'm keeping you from something then *do* let me know,' he ground out sarcastically. 'If not then perhaps you'd be so good to keep your mind on the job in hand.'

Verity glared as she slapped a swab in front of him. Sarcastic beast! He had been like a bear with a sore head all week ever since that ill-fated kiss on her sofa when they had decided, or rather *he* had decided, that he would take her and Sammi out on Saturday.

Tomorrow.

And if he was going to be in *this* kind of mood then, frankly, she was tempted to cancel it.

Except that she couldn't cancel it. It was not a date, subject to the whims of either participant. This was an opportunity for father and daughter to get to know one another. And it hadn't just been the father who had been driving Verity mad all week, either. Sammi had come a close second. Every sentence she spoke seemed to contain a question or a reference to my 'Daddy'. She had accepted the idea of Benedict being her father with such ease that Verity had felt positively guilt-ridden.

Wondering if she had been wrong to exclude Benedict for all these years. Once her temper had cooled down after finding him with another woman shouldn't maturity have taken over? At any time she could have tracked him down and told him and given him the opportunity to get to know his daughter from babyhood.

'Suction, please, Staff,' asked Benedict tone-lessly and saw Barney, the anaesthetist, pull an expressive face at his nurse. He could translate that half-amused look with complete accuracy. They wanted to know why the senior reg was in such a filthy mood.

And Benedict could tell them exactly why. The reason was a stunning blonde with the most amazing aquamarine-blue eyes and a body to die for and she was standing about three feet away from him, doing dangerous things to his blood pressure. What was more, she had been avoiding looking at him all day, which he couldn't quite decide was a good thing or a bad thing.

Why the hell had he done the gentlemanly thing the other night and stopped? Why hadn't he just made mad, passionate love to her? Imprinted himself on her mind and on her body so that she would never look at another man again.

You arrogant so-and-so, he thought as a rueful smile touched the corners of his mouth beneath the mask.

He closed the pelvic peritoneum over the vaginal vault and waited until his senior house officer had sucked away the excess blood and then swabbed at the wound before starting to suture the second layer of the abdominal wall.

He sighed as he closed the layer of muscle. It had been a long case. A long day. A long week.

Delicately he began to pull the needle through the bobbly yellow layer of fat which lay just below the skin. He had just performed a hysterectomy and bilateral salpingo-oophorectomy—the removal of womb, Fallopian tubes and both ovaries.

The woman in question was only thirty-two. An untreated bout of venereal disease in her teens had led to a chronic infection of her reproductive organs and she was infertile as a result. Benedict had sat with her for half an hour on the previous evening while the woman had sobbed her regrets for both past and future. And her fears that her boyfriend might leave her now that all chances of her having her own baby had gone.

He finished off suturing just below the skin line

with his distinctively swift yet skilful technique. At least the woman would have a neat scar, he told himself, but it was scant consolation. People thought of surgeons as cold and unfeeling—treating their patients like pieces of meat to be operated on. As though surgeons couldn't be touched by the tragedy which was a daily part of hospital life.

While the truth could not be more different—for Benedict, certainly. He never saw the patient in terms of just their illness and its surgical solution. He saw the patient as a whole person—there could be no other way for him. It was one of the reasons why he had achieved the highest marks ever recorded in his membership examination for entry into the esteemed Royal College of Obstetricians and Gynaecologists.

It was also one of the reasons why he had chosen the dual speciality of obstetrics and gynaecology.

Because when you were dealing with the obstetric bit—with pregnancy—you were for the most part dealing with young, healthy women. Cases like the other night—the maternal death—were exceedingly rare, thank heavens. And Benedict found dealing with childbirth a good counter-balance for the more depressing side of his work.

His houseman snipped the final suture and Benedict peeled his gloves off. 'Thanks very much, everyone,' he said, noticing that Verity had her head bent and was pretending to count a load of instruments on her tray.

Why the hell wouldn't she even *look* at him? he

wondered and flounced out of the theatre in the time-honoured style of the arrogant surgeon.

Verity watched him go, hating him and yet wanting him all at the same time. Dreading the next day's outing and yet almost ticking off the wretched moments until it arrived. And reminding herself of what it had been like the other evening when she had let him kiss her. She wondered how far she would have let him go had they not stopped.

No. She corrected herself hurriedly. *They* had not stopped. *He* had been the one to stop. *He* hadn't wanted to make love; she had. And she would do very well to remember that.

Verity pushed her trolley towards the sluice, glancing up at the theatre clock as she did so and thinking about Jamie and Harriet for the first time in days. With the time difference between here and the States they would probably just be getting up, she thought, her mouth softening with uncomplicated affection.

At that moment she really missed them.

'*More!*' Sammi yelled delightedly.

'More?' chuckled Benedict, heaving an exaggerated sigh of fatigue. 'You can't want more, surely?'

Sammi bobbed up and down in the turquoise water, her bright orange armbands blinding as she waved her plump arms around like a helicopter. 'I do! I *do*!' she declared and began to giggle excitedly as Benedict hoisted her up onto his broad, bare shoulders, down which the water from the swimming-pool trickled enticingly.

'Oh, let Benedict rest,' protested Verity, but only very half-heartedly. Her stomach ached from laughing; she could not remember laughing so much in years.

Benedict had called at the house at eight-thirty, a good half-hour before he was expected, and although the two of them were dressed they hadn't even had breakfast. In fact, Verity was about to scramble eggs.

'Would you like some?' she asked in a rather nervous and polite voice. She just didn't know how to act with him in a situation like this.

'No,' and he took the egg-box firmly out of her hand and put it on the side. 'It's your day off so go and get your coats on,' he instructed.

'But we're hungry!' objected Sammi.

He grinned, suddenly boyish. 'You and me both, sugar! And if you're good I might just buy you breakfast!'

It seemed particularly decadent to Verity to go out for breakfast, particularly when it was at the Grantchester Hotel in the middle of London's West End. They were given a table set amidst lush tropical foliage next to a vast swimming-pool and waitresses fussed over Sammi and seemed prepared to indulge their every whim.

'This is ridiculous!' Verity said crossly.

'What is?'

'Breakfast *here*—it must cost an absolute fortune.'

His green eyes held the light of genuine chivalry. 'Let me worry about the cost, Verity. Please.'

Put like that, how could she refuse? Verity stared down at a menu that was as long as her arm and glanced up to find Benedict studying her, an oddly satisfied expression on his face.

'So, what would you like?' he asked softly.

'Eggs?' she shrugged, rather helplessly. 'I just don't know how to choose between hens' eggs, ducks' eggs, quails' eggs or guinea-fowl eggs!'

He shook his head. 'You don't. First rule— never eat in a restaurant what you were going to eat at home!'

He thought she had quails eggs at *home*? 'You're making rules for me now, are you?' she challenged with a smile.

'Only for breakfast.' He gave one of his heart-stopping smiles. 'So let's have raspberries and blueberries. And croissants.' He crinkled his eyes at the waitress. 'And mango sorbet and a pot of coffee. Oh, and an iced cappuccino for the young lady.'

'Ooh! Thank you, Benedict!' cooed Sammi, casting an envious eye at the rather corpulent American businessman who was puffing his way up and down the swimming-pool.

Benedict saw the glance and interpreted it correctly. 'Do you like swimming?' he asked, and Sammi nodded her head vigorously.

'Because we could come back later and swim, if you'd like to?' And Sammi squealed her delight.

'I think that goes without saying,' commented Verity drily. 'But how can we come back? It's a hotel.'

'Oh, there's a sports club here,' he said casually, 'and I'm a member.'

And that would explain how he managed to have the kind of hard-packed, muscular physique which any self-respecting sportsman would be proud of, thought Verity. Though goodness only knew how much it would cost to belong to a place like this.

'But we don't have our costumes here,' Verity pointed out.

'There's a boutique in the foyer.'

And she could just imagine how much a swimming-costume would cost *there*. She opened her mouth but he anticipated her objection.

'Verity,' he said mock-sternly, 'aren't I allowed to spoil my daughter? And it wouldn't be fair to take *her* swimming and not her mother, now would it?'

For brazen charm he just about took the biscuit but Verity was enjoying herself too much to put up any objections. 'I suppose not,' she murmured.

'Good. That's settled, then.'

Under the guise of sipping at her fruit juice she allowed herself a good look at him. And she wasn't the only one. He was the kind of man who attracted looks from both men and women, even in a place like this where good looks and wealth were common enough to be unremarkable. He wore beautifully cut dark green cords, with a linen shirt in a much paler green. His tie was a silk affair—a rather wild explosion of peacock blues and greens which suited him perfectly.

He caught her looking at him. 'And do you approve?' he mocked.

She raised her glass to him. 'Best juice I've ever tasted!' she mocked back, and he laughed.

To Verity's pleasure the breakfast was followed by a walk in Hyde Park, where they threw scraps of stale bread to the ducks. She had been awfully afraid that he would provide such a packed, high-tech and expensive day that Sammi would be completely dazzled by it all. And she wanted Sammi to get to know him and to like him as a person and not for what he could provide for her.

In the event they stayed in the park for ages—there seemed so much new life to explore and see. Benedict had been planning to take them to a restaurant for lunch but when he suggested it Verity shook her head.

'It's such a glorious day,' she said. 'We don't get many like this. Can't we buy a sandwich somewhere and have a picnic?'

'Sure we can,' he replied but he frowned.

'Of course, if you really *want* to eat in a restaurant—' Verity began but he shook his head.

'It isn't that. It's just—'

Verity stilled. 'What?'

He shrugged in an effort to be light-hearted but his voice was grave. 'Oh, the mention of sandwiches made me think of Ethel. I got the results back from Histology last night. I'm afraid it's what I feared. She has adenocarcinoma of the body of

the uterus. I'm going to have to perform a
Wertheim's hysterectomy on Monday.'

Verity sucked in a breath as he mentioned
adenocarcinoma—a particularly virulent type of
cancer. And Wertheim's operation itself was
fraught with dangers. Suddenly it seemed very
important to comfort him, to take his mind off what
lay ahead of him. 'Let's walk,' she said suddenly.

Their eyes met understandingly. 'OK,' he
nodded.

They walked for well over an hour, briskly and
without speaking, Sammi happily skipping ahead
and depleting the park's daisy stock! The wind
whipped Verity's hair up and put roses in her
cheeks and she began to hum beneath her breath,
without being aware that she was doing so.

'Enjoying yourself?' asked Benedict.

His deep voice broke into her little daydream
and reminded her of how things were, not how
she would like them to be. He was walking close
enough for her to slip her hand into the crook of
his elbow, if she had chosen to do so. And that
was what she would have done if they *had* been a
proper family.

But they weren't, were they?

And, maybe, once Sammi was totally at ease
with her father it might make more sense for the
two of them to conduct their outings alone.

Because, sooner or later, Benedict *would* find a
woman he loved and wanted to settle down with
and if they carried on having carefree days like
this one then Verity might just build up a hopeless

emotional dependence on the man, one which he would never be able to fulfil.

But her good intentions went to pot later on when, after their swim, he took them to see a film. Verity was still a little breathless from the sight of seeing Benedict wearing nothing but a pair of very sleek, black swim-shorts. And even more breathless from the way he had been unashamedly admiring the shocking-pink Lycra swim-suit that she had chosen for herself—although she had had reservations about it. It was cut much too high on the leg to be decent but it also happened to be the only one in the shop in her size.

'Has she seen *Bambi* yet?' he asked, as the three of them studied the seven films showing at the giant complex.

'No. We've got the book.'

'Think she'd like it?'

'I think she'd love it.' She wasn't so sure about herself though. Verity could remember crying buckets the last time *she* had seen it—and that had been about fifteen years ago!

In the darkness of the cinema she tried vainly to eat the popcorn Benedict had bought but she found herself sniffing on more than one occasion and when it reached the bit about Bambi's mother dying she thought of Kathy and Jamie and Harriet and everything, really, and just dissolved. Benedict did nothing, except silently hand over a large, clean handkerchief and Verity was grateful to him for his tact.

She had managed to regain her composure by

the end of the film, although when the lights went up she thought that Benedict's own eyes looked suspiciously bright and she threw him a curious look.

'Disney was a master at blatant manipulation of his audience,' he observed laconically.

Verity hid a smile. 'Cynic!' she responded.

They took a black cab back to Verity's flat and Benedict looked down at his watch. It was still only seven and Sammi had fallen asleep on his lap. His heart warmed with pleasure as he stroked a silken curl from his daughter's cheek. Was it always going to be this easy to love her, he wondered? This simple?

He sneaked a glance at Verity, who was staring out of the window as all the famous London landmarks flashed by. When they reached her flat he would ask her out to dinner and if she couldn't get a babysitter then they would send out for something. He felt as nervous and as excited as a teenager on a first date.

He carried Sammi up to the flat and waited while Verity managed to get her into her pyjamas and into bed and when she came back into the room she brushed the back of her hand ruefully over her forehead.

'Whew!' she exclaimed, something in the way that he was looking at her making her babble in excitement. 'What a battle! I'm afraid that she's had to go to bed with her teeth unbrushed, not the best thing in the world when you consider the amount of sugar she consumed in the cinema. Still—'

'Verity—' he began, suddenly urgent, when the warbling of her telephone halted him.

'Excuse me,' said Verity quickly, relieved to have a reprieve. She knew what she had *said* she was going to do—not get her hopes up and play cool. But she had been wrong or deluded. Because if Benedict asked her out this evening, as she suspected he was about to, then she was almost certainly going to say yes.

'Of course,' Benedict answered. He went over to her bookcase and pretended not to listen, though naturally enough he could have recounted her end of the conversation word for word afterwards.

'Verity? Hi!'

'*Jamie!*' she squealed with delight. 'You sound so American!'

'Guess I do, y'all,' he drawled.

She laughed. 'How are you?'

'Exhausted! And frightened to within an inch of my life. Harriet insisted on dragging me on every infernal ride in the park today—including the ones which warned against it if you have a nervous disposition!'

'But you haven't *got* a nervous disposition,' Verity pointed out.

'I have now!' he countered, and she laughed again. 'Harriet wants to say hello to Sammi. Is she there?'

Verity swallowed, suddenly serious. 'She's in bed.'

'That's early.'

'I know. . .' Her voice trailed off awkwardly. Suddenly she felt stricken with guilt. 'Jamie,' she said, and didn't notice Benedict's shoulders tense.

'Listen,' said Jamie, as if he hadn't heard her. 'I'm coming home on Monday.'

'*Monday?*' Verity exclaimed. 'That soon?'

'I've been away almost a fortnight,' he reminded her gently. 'Didn't you miss me?'

'Yes, of course I missed you,' she replied truthfully.

Benedict quickly put the book down as if it had been contaminated.

'Can you meet me at the airport?' he queried. 'About seven?'

'How?'

'Take my car—my secretary will give you the keys.'

'Drive your *Jag*?' asked Verity disbelievingly. 'You trust me enough to drive *that*?'

'I'm the man who taught you to drive, remember?' he reminded her. 'Though I did have a sensible saloon at the time. Just go easy on the accelerator, right? Oh, and bring Sammi. Can you do that, Verity?'

'Sure I can,' she answered softly.

'Thanks.' He paused as if he was about to say something more but when he did it was nothing other than a casual, 'Bye for now.'

'Bye,' echoed Verity thoughtfully and slowly replaced the receiver to find Benedict staring at her, an oddly frozen look on his face.

'I'd better be going,' he said abruptly.

'Oh.' She tried to keep the disappointment out of her voice. 'Won't you stay for a drink? Or supper?'

He shook his head, trying to swallow down the black tide of jealousy that was sweeping through his veins like an illicit drug. 'No, thanks.' He picked up his jacket from the back of a chair. 'I have a paper I'm writing for the *Lancet*.'

'Benedict, it's been a lovely day—'

He couldn't bear it. To witness her formal little declarations of gratitude when all the while she probably wanted to work out what to wear to meet Jamie Brennan at the airport. 'Yes,' he replied, equally formal. 'I enjoyed it very much and I hope that Sammi did, too. I'll speak to you during the week about taking her out again. Maybe she might feel relaxed enough to come out with me on her own—give you a little free time. If that's OK.'

Verity nodded but it was an effort to prevent her face from crumpling. She had expected him to want to take his daughter out on his own, yes, just not this *soon*. 'That's fine!' she said brightly.

'Good. Goodnight, Verity,' and, turning swiftly away from her, he walked out of the flat without a backward glance, leaving Verity staring after him in bewilderment and dismay.

CHAPTER NINE

THE operating theatre was tense and crowded. Wertheim's Hysterectomy was still a rare enough operation to attract the various members of staff who would learn from seeing it performed. Thus there were medical students as well as all the O and G residents, not just from Jamie Brennan's team but also from the other O and G consultant's firm.

The fact that the patient was a member of staff, who was known and liked by them all, added an extra poignancy. Verity was nervous as she began to scrub up, her fingers shaking very slightly as she pumped the pink antiseptic soap onto her hands and her eyes closing briefly as she did something which she did not normally do before an operation commenced.

She prayed.

When she opened her eyes she found Benedict beside her, grim-set and sombre, and he nodded understandingly when he saw her face, her eyes like two startling aquamarines but lacking their usual sparkle.

'I'll do my very best,' he vowed, wishing that he had had the good sense all those years ago not to have let her go.

'I know you will.'

160

Unusually for Theatre, instead of the usual buzz of conversation there was a tense, expectant silence as Ethel was wheeled in and as Benedict walked towards the table, the student doctors parting like the Red Sea to let him through.

Verity handed him a swab to clean the operation site and then, as he took the scalpel blade from her, he said to the assembled watchers, 'This is, as I am sure you are aware, a much more extensive operation than a total hysterectomy. It is far more difficult and it takes much longer and the operative mortality and morbidity rates are much higher.' There was silence as he made the first incision. 'Any idea why?' he queried.

Ted Lyons, the houseman, answered. 'The dissection of the pelvis is very wide,' he said. 'And the patient may lose a lot of blood—thus the complications are shock, reactionary haemorrhage and fistulae.'

'And let's hope,' said Benedict quietly, as he sliced through the first layer of the abdomen, 'that we can avoid all three.'

Verity had only seen the operation performed once before and that had been by Jamie. And both men were extraordinary surgeons, although their techniques were fundamentally quite different. Benedict had the instinctive brilliance of the born surgeon, his decision-making often appearing erratic to the novice though he was rarely, if ever, wrong. He was one of those men who operated by touch as well as by sight, his long fingers deftly dissecting out the glands on the side wall of the pelvis.

Jamie, on the other hand, took longer. He was far more painstaking although he, too, was instinctive when he needed to be. No really good surgeon could survive without the ability to take risks. The difference was that Verity suspected that Benedict enjoyed the risks, whereas she knew that Jamie preferred to do without them.

The minutes ticked away. Benedict was fractious—she had never seen him so fractious. Twice he yelled at her. Once for handing him the wrong forcep. Except that it wasn't the wrong forcep. It was the one that he would normally have used. But today he wanted an instrument that Verity wasn't even sure they had in stock and she quickly sent Anna Buchan, her runner, off to investigate.

'And hurry up!' Benedict yelled.

The suction machine made a slurping noise. Verity glanced up at the clock. It was almost five o'clock. She should have been off duty half an hour ago and if she didn't leave soon then there was no way that she was going to be able to get to the airport at seven in time to meet Jamie.

While they waited for Anna Benedict saw her clock-watching and his temper, already held in on a tight rein, threatened to explode. 'If you have to be somewhere else, Staff,' he said coldly, 'then please arrange for another nurse to take over. I'd rather have someone more junior assisting me than someone who only has half her mind on the job!'

Verity didn't take it personally. She had a good

idea of the stress he must be under. 'There's no need for that, Mr Jackson,' she replied serenely. 'I'll stay until the end. Nurse Morris,' she called reluctantly, thinking that it was absolutely *typical* that she should have to relay this message to the biggest gossip in theatres.

'Yes, Staff?'

'Can you get someone to call the international arrivals desk at Heathrow and relay a message saying that Verity Summers will be unable to meet Jamie Brennan off his flight and that she apologises.'

'*Yes*, Staff!' answered Julia Morris, her expression eager.

Benedict forced himself to switch off from what Verity was saying, although tiny beads of sweat pricked his forehead before a nurse gently dabbed them away. This operation was tricky enough anyway, without letting his feelings distract him.

Anna returned with his forcep of choice and everyone breathed a collective sigh of relief.

By six-thirty Benedict was sewing up and the nurse went to dab at his forehead again but he shook his head impatiently, his mood unbearably black although the difficult operation had gone without a hitch.

'We're not out of the woods yet,' he told them. 'It could be several days or several weeks after the operation before we can safely say that there has been no damage due to interference with the blood supply to the ureter. Plus, this lady will have a tough course of radiotherapy to contend with. But at least the disease has not spread as much as I had feared. Thank you, everybody,' he said gravely, and took his gloves off.

By the time that Verity had cleaned up in Theatre and showered and changed it was almost seven-thirty and she rushed out of the changing room to find Benedict waiting for her in the empty corridor, grim-faced and brooding as he paced up and down.

She thought, rather stupidly as it turned out, that he might have been about to apologise for having been so abominably rude to her in Theatre, but no.

'I notice that you couldn't wait to get a message to your precious Brennan,' he sniped critically, his mouth hardening into an ugly line. 'Though I didn't detect the same kind of concern towards your daughter.'

Verity froze, as if unable to believe what she had just heard. 'I *beg* your pardon?'

'Where's Sammi now?' he demanded.

She made as if to push past him. 'That's none of your business!' she retorted, still shocked and still stung by his wounding words.

He stopped her. Literally. His fingers bit into the thin material of her jaunty yellow jacket. 'But that's where you're wrong, Verity!' he retorted. 'It just happens to *be* my business. You made it my business when you informed me that I was Sammi's father—and it might have been my business years earlier if you had had the courage to tell me!' he finished cruelly.

She stared at the hands, so strong and brown,

which still held her. 'Would you mind letting me go?' she said in a small, tight voice.

'Where's Sammi?'

'Where the hell do you *think* she is?' she demanded, her own temper spilling over now like a bulging sack of corn into which a knife had just been plunged. 'She's with the childminder, who I know and trust. Who knows me. Well enough to explain to Sammi that if I'm late, which I rarely am, that I am held up in Theatre. And, for your information, Benedict Jackson, whoever is in charge of the theatre suite has the childminder's number and knows to ring her if I *have* been delayed, as I was today.'

She glowered at him. 'And just because you're back in Sammi's life that doesn't give you some God-given right to try and take over—to try and criticise *me*! Not when you were the one who let us go!'

He gave her a bleak, hard look. 'But that's where you're wrong, Verity,' he said. 'I didn't let you and Sammi go. That decision was all yours.'

Tears began to slide down her cheeks. 'Take your hands off me,' she whispered.

He shook his head with a cold, clinical kind of detachment. 'Only if you let me run you to the childminder's.'

'Never!' she sobbed. 'Let me go, Benedict Jackson!'

He looked unmoved by her protestations. 'You're in no fit state to travel anywhere on your own and if you take public transport you'll make yourself unnecessarily late, which isn't really fair to Sammi, now is it?'

How dared he tell her what was or wasn't fair on Sammi? Where had he been during her pregnancy? During her long labour? And afterwards. Those nights when sleep had been at a premium and on cold, winter evenings when she used to go to bed at eight in the evening to save on the heating bills.

Too distraught to reason that she had brought her loneliness on herself, she sought to hurt him using the only method she had available.

'I can use Jamie's Jag!' she boasted, plucking the keys from her pocket and dangling them in front of his face.

He took them from her immediately. 'Not like that you can't,' he contradicted calmly. 'Quite frankly, I wouldn't put you in charge of a dodgem at the funfair at the moment, let alone one of the most powerful cars on the market!'

'I hate you!' she sobbed.

'Save your energy for your daughter, Verity!' he snapped, his patience at an end, and she lapsed into a hurt and indignant silence.

In the end she calmed down enough to appear relatively normal in front of the childminder but by the time that Benedict had driven the three of them home to her flat reaction had set in and she felt as weak as a kitten.

'Sit down,' he said, and he must have made her some coffee for a strong, steaming potful appeared on the table in front of her. 'And drink that!'

As she obediently sipped her coffee she was

vaguely aware that Benedict seemed to have everything under control and he had Sammi fed and bathed before she even realised it. When she stumbled along to the bedroom it was to find Benedict reading the last bit of *Bambi* to Sammi, whose eyes were almost closed and with a dreamy, contented smile on her face.

He gave her a don't-make-a-sound look and she nodded and went back into the sitting room, where he joined her a moment later. One look at the grave expression on his face brought her back down to a hard and unwelcoming earth.

For Verity was a nurse and a mother as well as a woman. And in that moment she recognised that some of his bitterness and hurt and resentfulness was justified. She *had* excluded him. It had been her choice.

She had not allowed Benedict the luxury of choice.

Tears welled up in her eyes. 'Benedict. . .' she gulped.

'Save it!' His mouth twisted as he took the keys to the Jag from the pocket of his jeans and dropped them contemptuously on the table in front of him. 'Here are the keys to your boyfriend's car—only, so help me, Verity, if I discover that you've gone anywhere near that car tonight then you'll have *me* to deal with.' His eyes glittered with anger. 'And I can assure you it will be an experience you will not relish!'

And, with that, he slammed his way out of the flat.

Verity slumped down on the sofa and started to cry and it was some time later that the phone began to ring and she snatched it up, praying that it was Benedict.

'Hello?' came Jamie's concerned voice when he received no reply. 'Verity? Are you there?'

'Oh, Jamie!' she sobbed brokenly. 'Jamie!'

'I'm coming over,' he announced grimly.

CHAPTER TEN

BY THE time that Jamie arrived Verity had managed to compose herself following Benedict's abrupt departure. She washed her face, changed into a dress and brushed her hair until it gleamed. Because it simply was not fair to Jamie to collapse weeping hysterically into his arms when he had just completed a long-haul flight and was very probably jet-lagged.

When Verity pulled the door open it took a good few seconds for her to recognise that it was indeed Jamie Brennan who stood there. It had only been a fortnight, she realised with a shock, but for a moment it felt as though she was looking at a stranger.

He was lightly tanned for a start and the colour made his blue eyes look all the more startling. And he had had his hair cut, too, while he had been away. Some groovy Californian hairdresser had obviously got to grips with the thick brown-black hair and had cut it slightly shorter than he usually wore it. It suited him.

He had obviously been shopping in America, too, because the suit he wore was not one that she recognised. More than that, her hobby was making her own clothes and she could tell from just a glance that the superb, almost casual, look was an off-the-peg number by one of the world's top designers.

He looked smart and preppy.

He looked sensational.

'Hi,' he said quietly, a fierce anger beginning to gnaw away at the pit of his stomach as he looked at her. Her face was as pale as paper—so pale as to be almost transparent, as if it was not blood that ran through her veins but some clear solution: tears most probably, he thought. She wore a short aquamarine linen dress he had seen before, which usually made her eyes appear as bright as jewels but tonight her eyes were red from crying.

And if Benedict Jackson had walked into the room at that moment then Jamie, not a man normally given to violence, knew that he would have punched him. Hard.

'Hi,' Verity echoed, an unbearable sadness suddenly swamping her, and her bottom lip began to tremble.

Jamie stared at her for a long moment and then gave an almost indiscernible nod and said something beneath his breath which sounded like 'yes'. His eyes looked dazzlingly blue but somehow lacking something and Verity wasn't sure what as he said, very gently, 'Aren't you going to invite me in?'

He followed her over the threshold, his eyes glancing around the flat as he searched for the signs of what he had most been dreading but there were none. So Benedict had not moved in, he thought grimly. Not yet.

'Shall I get us a drink?' she asked him in a wobbly voice.

He nodded. 'I could use one but I've a better idea. I'll get us one. You sit down before you fall down,' he added in a dry undertone.

Verity watched him as he disappeared in the direction of the kitchen for ice. He knew his way around her flat well; he had been there often enough. And yet she never felt as though he intruded or jarred. It wasn't like having an unexploded bomb in the room with you—like Benedict.

He fitted in so well with her life; he always had. They had the same tastes and the same impish sense of humour. Their daughters got on well together. If she sat down and wrote a list of all Jamie's good points and bad points she would be hard-pushed to find anything to put in the negative column.

Seeing him now with the fresh eyes that absence always created Verity realised for the first time how absolutely gorgeous he was. Tall and strong and handsome but—more than anything else—it was the immensely protective instinct which surrounded him like an aura that accentuated his good looks.

Why had she never noticed all these things before?

He handed her a gin and tonic, made exactly as she liked it with plenty of ice and a slice of lime floating decorously on the top.

She sipped it. Perfect. 'Where did you get the lime?' she asked inconsequentially.

'I brought it with me.' He managed a smile, harder to do at that precise moment than the hardest operation he had ever performed. 'You never—'

'Have any lime!' she finished for him on a gulp because he knew her so well and Jamie was too good a man to give up. She *wanted* to love him. So much.

He raised his eyebrows questioningly. 'So?'

'Tell me all about your holiday—'

But Jamie shook his head. 'No, Verity,' he said gravely. 'That isn't the reason why I'm here. Nor the reason why you were crying your heart out earlier. I wish that we could go back to what we were before—at least, at this moment I think I do—but we can't. Something has happened; something has changed—and I want to hear it from you.'

In a way it was a relief to be able to talk about it and Verity trusted Jamie so much. He had never been judgemental in the past and she knew that he would not be so now. 'I've seen Sammi's father!' she blurted out, not knowing what his reaction would be but certainly not expecting him to continue to sit there calmly sipping his drink, which he did. He looked at her with those startling blue eyes as he waited for her to continue.

'It's Benedict Jackson!' she announced, and then, when there was *still* no reaction, 'Your new senior registrar.'

'I see,' he said, still looking as relaxed as if he had just been given a message, though inside he felt as though honed razor blades were slowly nicking at his gut.

Verity put her glass upon the table and stared at him, something unfathomable about Jamie's response to what she was saying alerting her to a nagging disquiet. 'You don't seem surprised,' she commented astutely.

Jamie shrugged. 'Very little surprises me any more.'

'No. But it's more than that, isn't it, Jamie? It's—'

'No!' He cut across her stumbling response with a sharpness that was alien to her. Jamie, who had never raised his voice to her, now looked as though he was holding onto his temper with the most monumental of efforts. 'Before you ask me anything, Verity, let me ask you something. Do you love him?'

She didn't hesitate, although Jamie would have welcomed even the pretence of some hesitation. 'Yes. But he doesn't love me.'

'Doesn't he?' asked Jamie reflectively. 'Are you quite sure?'

Verity looked at him with renewed suspicion. Jamie was fairly unflappable, yes, but not *this* unflappable. 'You didn't know, did you?' she asked.

'Know what precisely, Verity?'

'About Benedict. Being Sammi's father.'

He risked her hatred now, but it was a risk he had to take for he was, above all, an honest man. 'Yes.' He saw her widened eyes and put his glass

down to stand beside hers in a cruel mockery of
partnership. 'I found out months ago——last year,
in fact. We were going skating. Do you remember?
And we forgot Sammi's bobble-hat. You asked
me to go back into the flat and get it. You said
you'd left it on top of the bureau.'

He paused. 'I found the hat all right, but you
had left the top drawer of the bureau open, and
inside I could see that silver cast you had had made
of Sammi's first shoe. I suppose it was sentimental
of me, but because Kathy had had one very similar
made for Harriet I picked it up.' His bright blue
eyes were rueful. 'And saw the photograph
underneath.'

Verity stared at him, and then nodded in comprehension. 'Of Benedict,' she said slowly.

'Of Benedict,' he agreed.

It was the one decent photo she had of him, with
his dark head thrown back with laughter, taken on
some glorious golden afternoon during their affair.
In the early days she had looked at the picture so
much that it had become rather dog-eared, and it
had been then that she had stored it away with her
most precious possessions, intending one day to
show Sammi a picture of her father.

Jamie gave a sad smile. 'It didn't require a detective to deduce that Benedict Jackson was her
father.'

The casual way he said Benedict's name
prompted her next question. 'And did you know
him?' she asked. 'Professionally, I mean.'

Oh, yes, he knew him. Once met, never forgotten; that was the brilliant, erratic Benedict Jackson. But Jamie's innate pride refused to let bitterness distort his voice. 'Yes, I knew him,' he answered quietly. 'And finding that out—well, it explained a lot. Your reluctance to discuss Sammi's father— that made sense, given Jackson's reputation.'

'His r-reputation?' stammered Verity.

Jamie could have kicked himself; she was the last person in the world he wanted to hurt. But she wasn't stupid, and he would not wish her to be naïve. 'He's played the field—but I guess you know that.'

Verity nodded. 'Yes, I know that. And, like I say, he doesn't love me so it's all pretty academic.' And then an idea began to form in her mind—a mad, crazy idea which, once it had taken seed, simply refused to stop growing.

'Jamie. . .when you saw Benedict's photo—the hospital hadn't even *advertised* for a new senior registrar at that time. . .'

'That's right.' Even in the midst of his anger and despair Jamie couldn't hold back a smile as he acknowledged her superb detective work.

'So you took Benedict on *because* he was the father of my child?'

'No!' he cut in quickly. 'I took Benedict on, *knowing* that he was the father of your child. There is a difference, you know, Verity. He was uniquely the best-qualified for the job; have no doubt about that.'

'But why didn't you *tell* me that he was coming to St Jude's? Why didn't you at least——?'

'I didn't tell you because I wanted you to confront the truth. It was important to me. I know that it was really none of my business but I felt, as a father myself, that he had the right to know about his child. I also felt that you ought to face your own feelings for Benedict—to know whether you still cared. But if you had known that he was coming there would have been time for you to build walls around yourself. You've been a princess in an ivory tower for long enough, Verity. Those walls had to come down some time.'

Verity blinked in confusion. 'But why? I mean, why was it so important to you?'

'Because my feelings for you had changed and I wondered if yours would ever change for me,' said Jamie simply. 'And I was confused myself. First you had been Kathy's friend and then *our* friend. And then, when she—' He leaned forward and took a mouthful of gin and tonic, then pulled a face. Would the day ever come, he wondered briefly, when he could mention the name of his wife without wanting to rail out at a God whose existence he sometimes doubted?

'When Kathy died,' he continued, 'you became *my* friend and Harriet's friend, too. And I badly wanted you to make the transition to becoming my lover. But we were too bound up in the past, both of us. That's why I took my holiday when Benedict was due to start; I thought it would kill two birds with one stone. That, perhaps, if I went away that you would miss me—'

'But I *did* miss you, Jamie!' Verity declared. 'Truly I did.'

He shook his head. 'Not the way I wanted you to miss me,' he smiled sadly. 'And, of course, I had hoped that you would discover that you had no feelings of love left for Benedict.'

She stared at him. 'That was a hell of a risk you took,' she said slowly.

'I'm a surgeon,' he shrugged. 'I'm in the business of taking risks. You win some; you lose some. Although you were never really mine to lose— you've always been in love with Benedict.'

'But I don't want to love him!' sobbed Verity helplessly. 'I want to love *you*!'

Jamie laughed, genuinely touched. 'It's a pity that we can't love to order, isn't it? The point is— what are you going to do about it?'

Verity raked her hands distractedly back through her hair. 'I told you—there's no point in doing anything. He doesn't love me—'

'You keep saying that,' broke in Jamie, unable to imagine anyone *not* loving this sweet, warm creature, 'but have you actually asked him *what* he feels about you?'

'Of course I haven't asked him!'

'There comes a time,' said Jamie patiently, 'when we have to let go of what went before— we have to—otherwise we aren't able to move on. Stop thinking about what Benedict did in the past or what *you* did. Think about now. How he is with you. And Sammi. If you don't give the man a chance, Verity, then you'll never leave your ivory tower. And it can be very lonely up there.' He stood up. 'And now I'm going.'

She stared at him as if for the last time, lingeringly and a touch longingly, but it was no good. Some women would have willingly settled for Jamie Brennan but she respected him too much to lie to him. And she *didn't* love him, not in the way he deserved to be loved.

While Benedict Jackson she *did* love—and she didn't have a clue about his feelings for her.

She sat in silence after he had gone and then, at last, Verity picked up the phone and punched out her babysitter's number.

It was about time that she started taking a few risks of her own.

CHAPTER ELEVEN

BENEDICT finished scanning the paper he had just completed, nodded his head and put it on his desk for posting then stared out of the window, stifling a yawn. The sky was still a delicate shade of eggshell blue overlaid with gold from the fading sunlight.

He felt like hell after his bust-up with Verity and sitting here was only going to make him brood over what she was getting up to with Jamie Brennan. It was a perfect spring evening; he ought to take a long walk and try and rid her from his system.

He had just pulled on an emerald cashmere sweater, bought for him by his favourite sister because she said it matched his eyes, when there was a hesitant knock at the door and he stifled a muttered curse. If it was that bimbo of a nurse from the floor below, thrusting her cleavage into his face one more time, then he really *would* have to tell her where to go.

He pulled the door opened and there stood Verity, all pale-faced and big-eyed and exquisite in some cool, understated dress. He found that he was examining her mouth closely. It didn't look all red and pouty as if Brennan had just spent the last couple of hours kissing her, he realised with a small sigh of relief. He suppressed the desire to

haul her inside and do that very thing himself.
Instead he raised an unfriendly eyebrow.

'Yes, Verity?' he enquired. 'What can I do
for you?'

Not too promising, thought Verity as she
attempted a smile. 'Can I come in?'

'Why?'

She was on the verge of cutting and running and
then she thought of ivory towers and taking risks.
'To talk to you, of course.'

He opened the door and gave a very passable
imitation of a mock-gallant, urging her inside. He
waited until he had closed the door before he asked
sourly, 'How did you get here? Did you bring your
boyfriend's car?'

'By cab,' she answered firmly, and then her
nerve deserted her and she wondered what she was
doing in this man's room when he was looking at
her as though he would like to throttle her or. . .
Her aquamarine eyes widened and darkened and
she saw a muscle flicker involuntarily in his cheek
as his body responded to her on some deep,
primitive level.

The first, faint glimmering of hope stirred in
Benedict's heart but he was wary, oh, so wary. For
he was acutely conscious of what he had found in
Verity and Sammi and he could not face losing
them, he could not.

Well, he might *have* to face losing Verity but
not Sammi. If Verity was going to marry Jamie
Brennan then he would have to learn to take it like
a man. He might not like it but it was the civilised

way to do things. The way people did things these days. Wasn't it? He stared at her steadily.

Verity took a deep breath. 'I want you to know that there's nothing going on between me and Jamie.' She paused and looked at him.

'And?' he enquired unhelpfully, though his heart had speeded up and was thundering like Niagara Falls in his ears.

Verity was beginning to wonder if she had made the most dreadful mistake. And then she saw the school photograph of Sammi that she had given him, standing in pride of place on his desk. He had had it framed in a heavily intricate silver surround. She gave it one last shot. 'I just—thought you'd like to know. That's all.'

'That's all?' he mused, as though she had just set him some interesting intellectual puzzle, and Verity lost her temper as she hadn't done in years. Not since she had been going out with Benedict, in fact.

'No, that's not all!' she yelled. 'I'm sorry that I kept Sammi away from you all those years. I was wrong and I want to make it up to you—'

'How?' he said immediately.

She shrugged. 'Well, I don't know—'

'I do,' he moaned. 'Come here. Please.'

She went to the kiss of a lifetime. On and on it went until they were both struggling to stay sane and Verity forced herself out of his arms before they ended up in bed. She had something more to say before they did.

'I don't know what you feel about me and at

the moment I don't care. I seem to have this problem where you're concerned, Benedict Jackson, in that you eclipse all other men and as this problem won't go away then I might as well just give in to it—'

He halted her by the simple expedient of placing his finger on her lips. '*You—don't—know—how—I—feel—about—you?*' he repeated slowly.

'It doesn't matter,' she mumbled, wanting to sweep the words away and be back there in his arms because only there did they not seem to hurt one another.

'Damn right, it matters!' he contradicted and sat her down very firmly in the chair by his desk. 'I love you, Verity Summers—'

'But you can't love me!' she protested. 'You've only been back a week—'

He frowned. 'Do you remember what Harold Wilson once said about a week being a long time in politics?'

She wrinkled her nose and attempted to joke. 'No, I don't think I do; I'm too young.'

He ignored that. 'Well, just think how long a day can be in hospital? Birth and death, joy and pain—every day. I think that a *day* can be a long time. And a minute was long enough for me to realise what I once so stupidly squandered. I want to protect you, to take care of you, to love you for the rest of my life.' And, to Verity's astonishment, he took her hand in his and said, very formally, 'So, will you please put me out of my misery and marry me, Verity?'

It was all too good to be true. 'No, I won't!' she howled. 'I'm not marrying you for Sammi's sake—'

Benedict nearly exploded. 'And I'm not asking you to—you stubborn woman, you! I'm asking you to marry me for love! *Love!*'

At that moment there was a loud thumping on the adjoining wall and a muffled, disembodied voice shouted, 'Just shut up, will you? Some people are *trying* to get to sleep!'

They stared at one another in stunned silence and then burst out laughing in unison and with the laughter fled the tension. 'This is where we came in,' giggled Verity. 'Hey! What do you think you're doing?'

Suddenly she was no longer on the chair but being put very firmly in the centre of Benedict's single bed.

'There is one way, and only one way, to subdue you, Miss Summers,' he announced with darkly exciting intent as he moved onto the bed.

'Oh?' Verity trembled with anticipation.

'Like me to show you?' he murmured.

'Yes, please.'

'Only if you agree to marry me. . .' His hand trickled from waist to hip.

'I'll only do that if you convince me that you love me.'

'And how do I do that?'

'You show me.'

*   *   *

Verity pushed her feet into slim cream leather shoes and flopped down in front of the mirror, exhausted.

'Don't sit down, Mummy!' scolded a small voice, and Verity caught sight of Sammi, resplendent in cream taffeta with an extravagant wreath of cream roses atop honey-coloured curls which now reached halfway down her back. 'You know that Auntie Sarah said you mustn't crease your dress!'

'What did Auntie Sarah say?' a voice trilled from the door and Benedict's youngest sister bounced into the room, looking a vision in a sleek-fitting dress in the same emerald green that she was so fond of buying for her brother. At twenty-four she was a dynamo—she even wore Sammi out!

'Mummy's creasing her dress!' complained Sammi.

'Shush, darling; go away and nag your daddy,' cooed her aunt, pressing an indulgent kiss on top of Sammi's head. 'He's next door, saying rude words to a poor, innocent little bow-tie!'

'Daddy's not *allowed* to say rude words!' his daughter announced with undisguised glee and the two women burst out laughing.

Sammi disappeared and Verity met Sarah's eyes ruefully in the mirror. 'How's it going?'

Sarah imitated someone cutting their throat. 'It's improved. Your father has finally accepted a drink—'

'Thank God,' breathed Verity fervently. 'How about Mum?'

'Oh, *she's* all right. Tickled pink that Benedict's finally making a decent woman of you.' Sarah waggled her finger reprimandingly at her soon-to-be sister-in-law. 'Although my brother assures me that he has asked you to marry him on a daily basis for the last two years. So what's happened to change your mind?'

Verity fastened the pearl necklace that Benedict's mother had given her and sat back to admire the milky lustre of the jewels glowing against her skin. 'Oh, I ran out of excuses.'

Sarah gave her a narrow-eyed look. 'No. I mean *really*.'

Verity hid a grin. Sarah was as persistent as her brother. In fact *all* his sisters were—all four of them—*and* their various offspring. She sighed. They had all agreed that the sprawling country house would make a spectacular setting for their wedding. And it *was* a wonderful, friendly house, overspilling with children and animals, but, *oh*, it was noisy!

Meanwhile, Sarah still looked in the mood for an explanation.

'It's because Benedict's just been made up to consultant,' Verity explained. 'I didn't think it would go down too well if the new pillar of the community was living in sin!'

Sarah grinned with pride. 'I know. Isn't it *wonderful*! St Thomas's, too, where you both trained—how romantic!' She hesitated. 'You know, Ben never did explain why you both transferred from St Jude's to Scotland so soon after he took up his post there.'

'Oh, a better offer came along,' answered Verity blithely, thinking how understanding the staff at St Jude's had been when the two of them had handed their notices in. But it would have been intolerable for her and Benedict and Jamie to have carried on working together, even though the two men had shaken hands, and Verity would always have a very special place in her heart for Jamie and Harriet.

'Do you know something?' mused Sarah. 'I could swear you're keeping something from me—'

'Time to vanish, little sister!' came a deep, amused voice from the doorway and Verity looked up to find Benedict standing there, tall and rangy and magnificent in a black tuxedo, tapered trousers and snowy shirt. Oh, and the rogue bow-tie—in place at last. His green eyes looked at her, so soft and loving that her stomach did its habitual flip.

'Go, Sarah,' he said softly.

'Oh, heck!' objected his sister. 'You're not going to start kissing her *again*, are you?'

'I might,' he drawled. 'If I could get a little privacy in this infernal house!'

'You leave for the church in an hour!' announced Sarah and gaily slammed her way out of the room.

He came to stand behind her, his hands resting

on her shoulders. 'Did I ever tell you how beautiful you are?'

'Not in the last half-hour!'

'Come here,' he instructed softly, 'and let me look at my bride-to-be properly. I won't be able to do this in church.' And he lifted her up and twirled her around, admiring the deceptively simple lines of the silk wedding gown that Verity, being Verity, had insisted on making herself. 'Or this,' he added and bent his head to kiss her.

'Benedict,' she whispered, when they came up for air.

'I love you, Verity,' he told her. 'Do you believe me now?'

'Mmm.' She had believed it after he had made love to her in that narrow hospital bed on the most beautiful May evening that she could remember. When he, too, had wept after discovering that there had been no other man for her in the intervening years. He had wished then that he could undo some of *his* past but of course he couldn't and they had both made a solemn vow to let the past go.

'That's the reason I've agreed to marry you,' she murmured. 'For love.'

'Is it?' he queried softly, and her cheeks became rosy as she hurriedly picked up the piece of parchment paper that was lying on the dressing table. She held it out to him. 'From Jamie,' she explained. 'I wrote and told him we were getting married.'

'Tell me what he says.'

'You don't want to read it for yourself?' she

asked in surprise and he shook his head gently.

'I trust you, sugar. And, what is more, I trust Jamie Brennan, too. So, what does he say?'

'Just that he's leaving St Jude's. He feels it's time to start anew. He's been offered a chance to head up the new research unit at Southbury Hospital, as well as take charge of the two O and G wards there. Thinks it'll be a great place to bring up Harriet, too.'

'It will.'

'Apparently, a friend of his works there—so at least he knows someone. A Leander le Saux.'

'I've heard of him,' said Benedict. 'A paediatrician of some repute. 'Now. . .' and he tilted her chin so that her gaze was captured in the green glory of his '. . .you were going to tell me—'

'What?'

'The real reason why you've agreed to marry me.'

'One,' she reached up on tiptoe to kiss him. 'I love you.'

'And two?'

She looked into the eyes of the man whom she had grown to adore more with each passing day. 'Is due around about Christmas-time.' She saw the laughter crinkling the corners of his eyes. 'Benedict Jackson!' she exclaimed perceptively. 'You *knew*! You knew all the time! You swine! You absolute swine. . .'

Downstairs, stuffing a smoked salmon sandwich into her mouth, Sarah raised her eyes heavenwards as she heard the muffled shouts and the long, long silence that followed them.

'Mum!' she called out resignedly. 'They're at it again!'

Look next month for
TAKING IT ALL, and find
out what happens to Jamie!
You'll love his story.

Heartbreak RANCH

Four generations of independent women...
Four heartwarming, romantic stories of the West...
Four incredible authors...

Fern Michaels
Jill Marie Landis
Dorsey Kelley
Chelley Kitzmiller

Saddle up with Heartbreak Ranch, an outstanding
Western collection that will take you on a whirlwind
trip through four generations and the exciting,
romantic adventures of four strong women who
have inherited the ranch from Bella Duprey,
famed Barbary Coast madam.

Available in March,
wherever Harlequin books are sold.

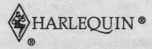

HARLEQUIN ®

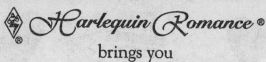

brings you

SIMPLY THE BEST

Authors you'll treasure, books you'll want to keep!

Harlequin Romance books just keep getting better and better...and we're delighted to welcome you to our Simply the Best showcase for 1997.

Each month for a whole year we'll be highlighting a particular author—one we know you're going to love!

Watch for:

#3445 *MARRY ME*
by Heather Allison

TV presenter Alicia Hartson is a romantic: she believes in Cupid, champagne and roses, and Mr. Right. Tony Domenico is not Mr. Right! He's cynical, demanding and unromantic. Where Alicia sees happy endings, her boss sees ratings. But they do say that opposites attract, and it is Valentine's Day!

Available in February wherever Harlequin books are sold.

FREE VALENTINE'S BROOCH! $9.95 U.S. retail value

This Valentine's Day Harlequin brings you all the essentials—romance, chocolate and jewelry—in:

VALENTINE Delights

Matchmaking chocolate-shop owner Papa Valentine dispenses sinful desserts, mouth-watering chocolates…and advice to the lovelorn, in this collection of three delightfully romantic stories by Meryl Sawyer, Kate Hoffmann and Gina Wilkins.

As our special Valentine's Day gift to you, each copy of *Valentine Delights* will have a beautiful, filigreed, heart-shaped brooch attached to the cover.

Make this your most delicious Valentine's Day ever with *Valentine Delights!*

Available in February wherever Harlequin books are sold.

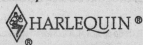

HARLEQUIN ®

Look us up on-line at: http://www.romance.net

VAL97